A Home Subscription! It's the easiest and most convenient way to get every one of the exciting Coventry Romance Novels! ...And you get 4 of them FREE!

You pay nothing extra for this convenience: there are no additional charges...you don't even pay for postage! Fill out and send us the handy coupon now, and we'll send you 4 exciting Coventry Romance novels absolutely FREE!

SEND NO MONEY, GET THESE
FOUR BOOKS
FREE!

C0981

**MAIL THIS COUPON TODAY TO:
COVENTRY HOME
SUBSCRIPTION SERVICE
6 COMMERCIAL STREET
HICKSVILLE, NEW YORK 11801**

YES, please start a Coventry Romance Home Subscription in my name, and send me FREE and without obligation to buy, my 4 Coventry Romances. If you do not hear from me after I have examined my 4 FREE books, please send me the 6 new Coventry Romances each month as soon as they come off the presses. I understand that I will be billed only $9.00 for all 6 books. There are no shipping and handling nor any other hidden charges. There is no minimum number of monthly purchases that I have to make. In fact, I can cancel my subscription at any time. The first 4 FREE books are mine to keep as a gift, even if I do not buy any additional books.

For added convenience, your monthly subscription may be charged automatically to your credit card.

☐ Master Charge
42101

☐ Visa
42101

Credit Card #_____

Expiration Date_____

Name_____
(Please Print)

Address_____

City_____ State_____ Zip _____

Signature_____

☐ Bill Me Direct Each Month **40105**

Publisher reserves the right to substitute alternate FREE books. Sales tax collected where required by law. Offer valid for new members only.
Allow 3-4 weeks for delivery. Prices subject to change without notice.

SWEET DISORDER

a novel by

Claudette Williams

FAWCETT COVENTRY • NEW YORK

SWEET DISORDER

Published by Fawcett Coventry Books, a unit of CBS Publications, the Consumer Publishing Division of CBS Inc.

ISBN: 0-449-50206-6

Printed in the United States of America

First Fawcett Coventry printing: September 1981

10 9 8 7 6 5 4 3 2 1

dedicated to my husband, Gordon,
who is ever, sweetly, disorderly,
very much my love. . . .

Chapter One

*A dainty and elegantly shod foot tapped impa-*tiently against the oilcloth that covered Squire Ingram's cozy library floor. Green eyes glared militantly as Miss Venetia Tay rounded on the young man standing before her.

"Don't try to fob me off, Ferdy, for I won't have it!"

The Honorable Ferdinand Skillington looked at the goddess of his affections and responded with horror, "But . . . Van, got it all wrong. Not trying to fob you off . . . trying to make love to you."

Venetia stopped her tapping foot and regarded her younger brother's lifelong friend in some surprise. He was no more than twenty, fair, lean and so well dressed she had always thought he aped the dandy set. He twirled his top hat nervously in his gloved hands, and she realized all at once that

7

he was in earnest. She stifled her surprise and her amusement and patted his hand with a resigned sigh.

"Are you, Ferdy? You shouldn't be." She waved off the remark that sprang to his eyes and would have emitted from his lips had she not cut him off. "But never mind. Those things usually have a way of righting themselves. Look, Ferdy . . . I know that my brother is up to something, but I can't figure out what it is." She frowned over this. "Gilly has never before been so secretive, so don't try shamming it, Ferdy. I want you to tell me what Gilly has been at."

Ferdy gulped to see his beloved so distressed. The truth of it was that Gilly had not taken him into his confidence, and though he had some notion of what his friend was up to, he didn't feel it was the honorable thing to go blabber about it to his friend's sister. "Aw now, Van . . . I really think you are making too much of this. Depend upon it . . . he is just larking about."

She shook her head. "No, he is embroiled in something dreadful. I feel it." She looked into Ferdy's pale-blue eyes with such a sorrowful look that he was moved to step forward and hold her shoulders firmly in his grip. Gently she removed herself. "You see, for the first time in his life, he has lied to me . . . and it was a regular out-'n' -outer. Oh, Ferdy . . . I have this miserable sinking feeling . . ."

"No, no . . . with the squire abovestairs ready to move out . . ." He bit his lower lip. "Well, what I mean . . . the squire being so ill and all has you in a fidget. No wonder."

Venetia's eyes clouded over. She looked imploringly up at him. "Ferdy . . . I entreat you to tell me what he is about. Or if you feel you can't do that, at least try and keep him from getting into mischief."

With more boyish eagerness than grace, Ferdy bent and passionately kissed Venetia's ungloved hand. He was in the very midst of his very first affair of the heart, and all his intentions were as pure as the platonic notions he held. "I promise you, Venetia, that I shall do my best." He came up from her hand, and as a sudden thought grabbed him he added with a frown, "Gilly won't like it, you know."

Miss Venetia was moved to chuckle. "Be discreet, Ferdy . . . don't let him know you're concerned." Then, with a sigh, "Now off with you, for I have some things I have to attend to."

"And that's another thing, Van. The squire has no right working you here like a housekeeper. Why, you run the place . . . and it ain't the thing, you know. You ought to be in London." However, it occurred to him that if she were to go to London she would find herself besieged by any number of suitables, and that competition he could not at the moment contemplate. "At any rate, you should be allowed out more."

"Ferdy, I get out as much as I wish to. But with the squire so ill I just can't . . ."

"Fudge!" retorted Ferdy.

Venetia laughed good-naturedly and ushered him out of the library. She turned back to the room with a long sigh. The chill of October was setting in, but the squire didn't want fires set until evening. She had already broken the rule and set a very small one in the grate. It was burning out. Hang it all! She was going to set another log on. After all, she was expected to work the books, and she would do so in some aura of comfort! She threw a sturdy pine log into the large and ruggedly designed hearth and then went to her desk.

Quill was held poised and ready as she resigned herself to a morning's work with the household figures, but for no reason at all she thought of her mother. Another time swelled in her memory. She had been a little girl, peeping around the ballroom door as her mother swirled in her father's arms and fashionable people frolicked. All that was past. Both parents were gone, as was the comfortable living her father had gambled away. Squire Ingram never let her forget that, and often was the time he called her her father's daughter. "If it wasn't for me, young lady," he would say forebodingly, "you'd go the way of your father!"

Ah me, she sighed to herself. She shouldn't feel so ungrateful toward her late aunt's husband, but she did. He was mean-fisted, and cold-hearted. There was no other way of describing him. She was twenty-three now, nearly a spinster, but when she had hinted at a London Season, he had laughed harshly and told her she had better take up the vicar's offer, for there would be no Season for her! And then he had behaved oddly, looked at her intently.

"Never mind the vicar if you have a disgust of him, dear," he had said. "I'm not a cruel chap."

"No, of course you are not," she had answered

politely. He had, after all, been footing the bill for Gilly and herself these past six years.

"No, that's right ... and there is m'heir, you know."

"Taylor?" she had shot back at him quickly. "Don't be absurd. We don't even like each other. Uncle ... Taylor isn't interested in me."

"Don't be talking slum at me, girl! If he isn't interested, it's because you ain't made a push in his direction! Taming, that's what Taylor wants."

"That may be so, squire, but I am not the girl to try it," snapped Venetia, her temper on the rise. She expected a quick reprisal from him, but none came. Instead he gazed at her long and thoughtfully.

"Off with you now, girl, you tire me ... you always tire me."

She got to her feet and left. He had a way of taking her off guard. He had done it just now, for a flash of affection had entered his weary old eyes. She left his room and thought no more about the conversation. Perhaps a flickering thought of his lordship Taylor Westbourne came to mind, but it was quickly dismissed. His lordship had always seemed an arrogant, selfish, hedonistic and conceited rake.

And then that very evening the squire had suffered a devastating attack.

All sorts of things had happened. He had sent for his man of business, and dispatches were posted ... and Gilly, there was Gilly acting so strange. Until the other night she had thought it was the high spirits of a youth home from Cambridge ... but a look at Gilly's guilty eyes when he had lied to her, and she was sure he had lied to her, told her he was playing deep. What to do?

In the Highlands of Scotland, where everything is sky, and vast treeless grasslands and moors, where life is hard and history full of legends created around the great clans, a castle in its last dregs of ruins crumbled in sad residence. It was a monument to a past long put aside.

The lord of this castle, Iverness, Charles Mac-Gregor, paced in one of the last few habitable rooms. His hazel eyes flickered as he stopped before his long, wide window and gazed out on the loch. It was all so beautiful, and for an unguarded moment he wanted to raise his hands to the sky in savage repudiation of what was happening to his home.

Most of his valuables, treasures handed down from father to son over the centuries, were now gone. Disposed of in order to pay his debts, in order to keep this his last hold on the past. His ather had ruined the last of their hopes by marrying without financial advancement in mind. Oh, Charles's English mother had brought to verness a handsome enough settlement, but she had been English . . . and her settlement had not gone far enough. He swept his auburn curls impatiently.

A knock sounded on the huge heavily brassed oak door. Charles turned and admitted his man, one of the few remaining servants.

"What is it, Mulby?"

The man bowed respectfully and presented his ordship a silver salver. Atop it was an ivory envelope, "It comes from the laigh, it does . . . that English relative of yourn."

"Really?" said Charles, his eyebrow up. He had been very meticulous with his visits to Squire Ingram. Here was his only chance. The squire was reputed to be a wealthy man, but too often he had received the impression that his uncle was not overly fond of him. What then was this? He took up the envelope, broke the seal and scanned the short contents with interest. Slowly, very slowly, his lips curled.

"Mulby, pack my things. We have quite a journey ahead of us."

"Ock no, is it to London then, me laird?"

"No, we will be booking passage on the stage for Northumberland. We are off to my uncle's, and, I think . . . good fortune at last!"

Squire Ingram was the last of his name. He had had three sisters, all gone now. The eldest of these had married her Highland Scotsman, MacGregor. She had been the least favorite of the squire's sisters, and Ingram had been quite put out by her marriage to a penniless Scot. From time to time, after her husband's death, he had sent her enough cash to keep her and her only son, Charles, out of debtors' prison, but he had resented the expenditure bitterly.

The second of his sisters had been another who had set up his back, with her marriage to a military gentleman whom the squire had taken in dislike. However, she had managed very well without his brotherly help and had produced, after many miscarriages, a lovely girl, Francine.

Francine Fenton had lost both her parents while her father was doing a military tour in India. They had fallen victims to Asiatic cholera and had not survived its ravages. Friends of her father's had seen her safely back to England, where she had gone into the care of her father's mother. Francine's grandmother coddled, caressed, and preened over her. She was much in her father's likeness, tall, with golden-brown hair and large blue eyes. Her father's small but comfortable living was matched with a nature placid enough not to make her hanker after more.

However, her grandmother had great ambitions for her. Such a beauty deserved, she felt, no less than a duke, or at least an earl. She had in her favor to promote such a match a granddaughter who was quite, quite lovely, but what she needed for Francine was a larger dowry.

These thoughts bumped one another in her head, as she gazed at her granddaughter, serenely embroidering near the fire. Her butler presented her with a sealed missive.

She took the letter from the salver before her and dismissed him as she put up her spectacles and surveyed the contents. A frown eased itself across her features, but it was not a look of displeasure. Here was the answer to all her dreams, but there were obstacles. She was not well enough to travel, and Northumberland was quite a distance. It would take a week.

"Francine, darling, how would you like to go pay a visit to your Uncle Ingram?"

Francine had met him only once, and it had been a meeting that had left her with a hazy notion of an unpleasant man. She wrinkled her nose. "I don't think so, Grandmama."

"No, child, I don't really blame you for that, but what if I told you it would particularly please me?"

She cocked her head. "Oh . . . then of course, Grandmama."

"Dearest child. I shall send you with your maid, and for the journey we shall hire your own private chaise. Would you like that, love?"

Francine Fenton had not the least desire to travel, to experience adventure. One might remember that as a child she had had quite enough of it with her volatile parents. She was, however, a sweet being very desirous of pleasing. "Yes, Grandmama, that would be very nice."

The youngest of the Squire's three sisters had been a lively creature, full of naughty wit, mischief and charm. Squire Ingram had soured over the long years of disillusionment, yet even so, he had never been able to squelch the smile that would flit into his eyes when he chanced to think of his youngest sister. She had had a way of always wheedling herself into his affections with the open adoration she was never loath to lavish on him. She had a way of drawing out a grin with her constant teasing. And then she had the good sense to marry Lord Westbourne, a man of rank and good ton. The squire had approved heartily of the marriage, and therefore it was not an odd thing that he held both her male offspring in some esteem.

Lord and Lady Westbourne were a popular pair,

well loved by their peers. However, neither one had a groat of economic sense. It wasn't long before they were badly dipped. Westbourne did not turn to the squire for help, but instead he had mortgaged his vast estates and was thus able to jaunt merrily along with his frivolous wife.

The first of the Westbourne lads had joined the Horse Guards. A plucky youth, he had gone off to Spain and fought Napoleon. His efforts won him the rank of major. And then suddenly, London's haut ton went off to Brussels to watch their army beat Napoleon at Waterloo. Westbourne's eldest son was lost in that battle, and his lordship and Lady Westbourne were killed in a driving accident very near the battle. This left their youngest son, Taylor, the title and the responsibilities of an indebted estate.

Waterloo was nearly three years past. The present Lord Westbourne had endured the death of his parents and elder brother, but it had left a tarnished man, where there had once been a playful scamp. He was now thirty years old, bored with life and cynical about society's baubles.

He had inherited the title and an encumbered estate. He saw the female of his choice, the star that glittered in his eyes, the form that made his heart pound, married to another whose estates were not mortgaged, and he hardened still further. So he turned inward and began the management of his holdings with earnest application. It proved slow, but rewarding, and then a distant aunt left him a small fortune.

Perversely, contrarily, he kept it a well-hidden secret. This was possible because he never dipped into its immense hold, but chose instead to pursue his goals by enlisting his sharp mind. A small but wise investment here, another in the funds from the profits of the first, an educated wager on a horse he had trained for Ascot; these things were pushing him forward and out of debt.

His lodgings were modest bachelor rooms situated off Pall Mall. His study was an odd assortment of old furniture that held little of style or grace, but were immensely comfortable. A collection of guns both modern and antiquated lined one faded wall. On another, various paintings of his late family were gathered, and over the small fireplace was a large, ornately framed mirror into which various calling cards had been stuck.

In the center of the dimly lit room, for only one window overlooked the street, was a desk of some size and usefulness, a gothic piece saved from the sale of his family's town house some months before. Behind the desk sat his lordship, contemplating a stack of ledger sheets. He had compiled enough capital to make several well-thought-out investments, and as he attended to his paperwork, his valet entered the small and cozy room.

The small man came forward and, discovering his employer deep in thought, caught his attention with a deprecatory cough,

"Hmmm . . . my lord . . ." said the valet gently. He proffered a silver tray, upon which rested a sealed envelope.

"Oh, hello, Timms, what have you there?" said Westbourne absently.

"Sorry to interrupt you, my lord, but this did just come by special post."

"Special post?" repeated Westbourne. His gray eyes glanced over the envelope as he took it in hand. His dark brow arched high as he noted the style of his uncle's hand.

"Well, well ... I wonder what Squire Ingram has to say."

Timms puzzled over the problem. The last time they had received a missive from the squire, it had sent his lordship hotfooting it to Northumberland. The timing had been bad, for it had been only months after Westbourne had lost his family at Waterloo. He found himself experiencing a sinking feeling of dread.

Westbourne perused the letter without smiling. Its contents were brief and to the point. He held his uncle in some affection and he did not like to deny Ingram, but the squire's request came at a bad time. It drew an oath out of him.

"Damn!"

"Trouble, my lord?"

"My uncle writes that he is unwell and wishes me at his side as soon as possible." There was nothing for it, he would have to go.

"Shall I pack your things, my lord?" Timms was resigned.

"I am afraid so, old boy. It can't be helped. When you send around for my carriage, have my groom hitch up my chestnut as well. I shall want a mount to break up this tedious journey."

"Yes, my lord." Timms sighed.

Westbourne stared blankly as his valet went off to do his employer's bidding. Squire Ingram had always treated him with a strange and very often harsh attention. In this treatment, Westbourne had always sensed affection and had responded in kind. How often had he heard his uncle compare him with his mother? He couldn't ignore his uncle's plea, but it was the devil's own timing! Could it be that his uncle was again playing off one of his stunts? To what purpose?

The last time Ingram had sent for him, it had also been on the pretext of bad health. That had been nearly three years ago, and he had gone dazed and aching over his brother's and parents' death. He had been in the midst of dangerous waters with debts ringing all around. Now, things were quite different.

He restudied his uncle's letter. It portended something more than the words he read, but what? His uncle hinted at the inheritance he stood in a position to receive. He smiled to himself. Of course—Ingram, like everyone else, thought him still in need of money. Well, well, he would go up to Northumberland and play his uncle's game. It might prove to be diverting after all.

Chapter Two

When it came to his home and his horses, Squire Ingram was most generous, but he was miserly about many things. As Venetia tooled the high-stepping pair of matched chestnuts down the long winding drive that led to the elegant sixteenth-century manor house, this thought occurred to her most forcibly. Why then had he suddenly sent her on a shopping spree? There was no denying the fact that he had colored up with the effort, but send her off he had, and with strict orders to choose gowns in the highest kick of fashion. Why?

Sweeping lawns of rich trim green waved in rolling splendor as she rounded the bend. She could now see the weaving River Tweed in the distance, and there, there was Gilly! She had been wanting a word with him all day, but somehow he had managed to avoid her. She watched a moment

21

as he cast his fishing pole in the dark smooth water and smiled. He looked a mere boy with his yellow hair massed about his charming face. She drove to the stable and nimbly jumped down from the open curricle, giving the reins to a young black groom.

"Tend them, Josh, and have someone take up the packages to the house. I shall go up presently."

"Yes, miss, but the squire, he been calling after you these twenty minutes and more."

"Has he? On well, then another ten minutes won't make a difference." She smiled, picked up the skirts of her serviceable brown habit and hurried off down the hill to the riverbank that flirted with Ingram lands.

Mr. Gilbert Tay sat crouched on a weathered log, his fishing line swaying in the river before him. He glanced up at the sound of her approach and grinned wide. "Hello, Van . . . buy out Mrs. Brant's dress shop?"

She chuckled. "Very nearly. I don't know what came over the squire, Gilly, but I thought I had better make good work of his lapse."

Gilly frowned suddenly and turned back to the river. She sat beside him and touched his shoulder. "What have I said, Gilly? What is it?"

"It's just that I hate having to grovel to him. I hate your having to do without . . . and I hate having to wait till I'm twenty-five to do right by you, Van. Good Lord . . . by then you'll be an old maid and past launching!"

She put her hands on her hips in mock anger. "Well! I like that!"

He peeped sheepishly, "You know what I mean.

I want to give you a Season now, Van. You deserve it. But with my inheritance all tied up until my twenty-fifth birthday . . ."

"Never mind. It doesn't matter."

"But it does. Dash it, Van, you may be my sister, but I got eyes in m'head and I can see you are a beauty. It isn't right you being shut up here. You should go to London . . . and damned if I don't manage it!"

She gazed at him thoughtfully. "And how, Gilly, just how could you manage it?" She was most serious now, for this brought her to what worried her most about his doings.

"That's not for you to worry about!" he said roughly. "I won't be questioned like a child, Van."

"No, I didn't think you would." She decided to drop the subject, for he looked obstinate, and there was never any moving him when he got into such a mood. She sighed and rested back on her hands.

"It is so lovely here though, Gilly . . . it has almost made missing a London Season quite forgivable. And you know, there is the vicar . . . and Ferdy . . . paying me court." There was the tease in her green eyes and her tone.

He laughed. "Haven't you told Ferdy to take a damper yet, Van?" He shook his head. "If ever there was a noddy . . . I mean . . . you and Ferdy?" This sent him off into a peal.

"And don't forget the vicar!" she put in.

He sobered. "You are not thinking of tying the knot with him, are you, Van?"

"Don't you like him, Gilly?"

"Oh, as to that, he is a decent sort, I suppose,

but hang me if he don't have a habit of prosing on forever." He considered the matter. "No, he would never do for you, Van . . . and I tell you what. Know why the squire sent you off after all that finery?"

"No, why?"

"Means to settle you on one of his nephews! Heard it from Groomsby."

"Oh no, you cannot mean it, Gilly! That is dreadful. I won't have it."

"Don't worry, Van. He can't make you marry either of them. You have me to stand buff for you . . . and I have already said I mean to launch you properly, *in London*. Depend upon it!"

For a lad who wished his sister's curiosity abated, this was a singularly unwise thing to say. However, just as Venetia frowned and started to again question him, a male voice at their backs brought their heads around and drew a low groan from Gilly.

Venetia smiled a welcome at the somberly-clad gentleman making his way toward them. The vicar, John Qerkdon, was not an unattractive man, but more often than not his pleasant good looks were overridden with a grave expression of thoughtfulness. When one considered that such a look usually preceded a long diatribe of metaphysical philosophy, it was easy to understand why Gilly whispered, "Send him off, do, Van . . ."

"Hush." She waited for the vicar to descend the slope and called out amicably, "Hello . . . have you come from the house, John?" They had been on friendly terms since the squire had chosen to appoint the young minister some three years ago.

Vicar Qerkdon frowned at Gilly. He had always found Gilly Tay a young lad too much given over to levity. He did not approve of the way his sister had of doting on him.

"Gilly, how can you keep your sister sitting on that damp log?"

Gilly flushed darkly and mumbled something about Venetia's being comfortable enough.

"Oh yes, John, I quite love it out here, you know, so don't be blaming Gilly."

"Well, that is very like you, Venetia, coming to his defense."

She stood up and said on a low, very nearly angry note, "Now, John, have you come to quarrel with me . . . or walk with me?"

John Qerkdon was thirty-two years old. He had, he believed, conquered most of his youthful fancies, but Venetia was a weakness with him. Her smile, her eyes, her voice had a way of moving him in a manner no other before her had ever done. Something deep inside him said, Beware, beware, she will run you ragged, laugh at your gravity. Egad, she was doing it now! Still, he gave her his arm and allowed her to wield him.

"You know that I could never quarrel with you, Venetia." His voice was low, soft. He would make her his wife and curb her giddiness.

She looked away, all too aware of his meaning. "Did the squire receive you?" she said to change the subject, and plucked at a yellowing leaf and gave it to the breeze.

"No, I did want to speak with him, but he sent word that he wasn't receiving." He was frowning again. "Venetia . . . you know what it is that I want to discuss with him?"

"No, how can I?" She laughed lightly and searched her mind for a subject to divert him, "But tell me, John, do you think he can be quite himself?" There was a tease in her green eyes, in her tone, that mocked the question.

He picked up on it and smiled. "Now, why should you ask?"

"Well, you must know he sent me on a shopping spree. Commanded me to furbish my wardrobe with the latest London styles, even demanded that I crop my hair in the newest fashion." She was gurgling pleasurably, for fresh in her mind was the assortment of gowns she had chosen from the *Fashion Plates*.

"Gadzooks!" the good vicar was moved to declare, after which he flushed and caught himself up. "Er . . . what I mean is . . . well, never thought the squire had a mind . . ."

"To hand over the blunt for such trifling things?" she supplied unmercilessly.

"Yes, no, that is . . ."

She laughed out loud and tossed her head with the sound. Her long bright hair of white-gold blew in the breeze away from her face, and the vicar could not help but fall beneath her spell. "Gilly thinks he means to impress his nephews. What do you think?"

He opened his light-blue eyes wide, "His nephews? Never say he has sent for them?"

"Well, he *has* been unwell." She grew suddenly very serious. "And John . . . I honestly do not think he will recover from this latest attack."

He patted her hand. "There, there, Venetia . . . you have me to see you through this."

She looked at him for a long moment and suppressed a heavy sigh. Indeed, she had Vicar John. . . .

The kitchen at Ingram Place was situated in the east and took in the morning sun through its long, wide, lead-paned window. It was a warm, bright room where most of the household staff would gather sooner or later and discuss the woes of the day. However, it was an acknowledged thing that Cook and her husband, the butler Groomsby, reigned supreme.

A chambermaid carrying a heavily laden tray came through the spring doors, set her tray by the washbasin table and brushed a wayward strand of hair away from her eyes. "Lordy, but the squire is in a feisty mood this morning. Nearly threw the hot chocolate at me. Would have, too, if Miss Venetia hadn't managed him."

Groomsby's sparsely covered head of gray came up, and he looked at the young girl. "Was she sitting with him, then?"

"Naw, more's the pity . . . that other was with him, reading." The girl's eyes went to the ceiling in a fashion that clearly indicated her opinion of such goings on.

Miss Francine had arrived two days earlier, and all the household staff seemed bent on picking up the cudgels on Miss Venetia's behalf. Not that she needed such defense. Not that she wanted such defense. Not that she even realized such a war was presently engaged, for she had taken to Miss

Francine and was heartily glad of another female near her own age.

The household staff did not feel the same way, for they had heard the squire call Miss Francine a diamond of the first water, a term he had never used in describing Miss Venetia. Fists started to form. They had heard the squire tell his solicitor that he was very much tempted to leave everything he had to such a fine specimen of feminine sweetness. Fists came into position.

Miss Venetia was their accepted, their adored, mistress of Ingram Place. She saw to the even running of the estate. She saw to the well-being of the squire's staff. Why, Bess could remember when nearly the entire household was abed with quinsies and it was Miss Venetia herself who tended to most of them.

"Reading, was she? As though she could!" declared Bess feelingly. "She is a simpleton, that's what, and if the squire don't see it, then he is less a man than even I took him for!"

"Now, now, Bess darling . . . don't get your bristles up. It won't do no good. Miss Venetia knows well enough how to handle the squire." He thought about this as he sipped his tea. "I'll tell you whot . . . it's a deep game himself is playing . . . drawing us into it, I think."

"Now, Groomsby . . . what can ye mean by that?" asked his astonished wife.

"Mayhap his remarks were meant for our ears. Think on it," answered her husband portentously.

"That don't fadge," said his wife.

"Well, we'll see . . . we'll see. And Lord bless me if that isn't another carriage coming up the drive." He got to his feet and hurried off. His wife, ladle in hand, stood a moment and watched his departure. He was a knowing one, her Groomsby, but just what did he mean?

The objects of all this concern sat in perfect harmony with one another in the drawing room. Francine chatted happily about her London Season, about the fashions, the gossip and the hopes of her grandmama, which prompted Venetia to ask:

"Why, Francine . . . you don't seem very enthusiastic about . . ." She laughed lightly. *"Trapping a catch!"*

Francine leaned forward onto her knees and put the sampler she had been stitching to one side. "That is just it, Venetia. I don't want a catch. I should not be comfortable at all with the Duke of Malmesbury!"

"Oh dear . . . and would your grandmama force you into such an alliance?"

"Oh no . . . in fact, the duke has not come up to scratch yet. That is why I am here."

"Is it? I don't understand," said Venetia, wrinkling her nose in a style peculiar to herself.

"Well, Grandmama feels that if my dowry . . . my expectations . . . were grander, the duke might find it more acceptable to propose."

"Oh! He must be an odious person!" exclaimed Venetia, who in spite of her twenty-three years was still green in such matters.

Francine examined this point of view doubtfully. "But Venetia, it is the way of the world," she said gravely.

Venetia released a light trill of laughter. "Look who is talking, you innocent. What do you know of the world?"

"Not very much, but I do know that a girl cannot make a desirable match without a dowry."

"Yes . . ." said Venetia, frowning. "I suppose that is the sad truth of it." She sat thoughtfully for a moment before posing her next question to the younger girl. "What then are you going to do, Francie? I mean . . . if he does come up to scratch?"

Francine shook her head. "I don't think about it . . . though it might be nice to be duchess. At least, Grandmama says it would." She screwed up her mouth as she imagined what this might entail. "But Venetia . . . it wouldn't suit me. I am persuaded I would be dreadfully unhappy. I don't like the notion of running a large house and having a flurry of servants to handle and . . . oh, you know, all the things a duchess would be expected to manage."

"Then tell your grandmama you won't have the duke."

"I can't do that. She would be so miserable." She brightened then. "Never mind, though. The squire might not leave me all his money, and then the duke would not propose."

Venetia laughed at this ingenuous remark and got to her dainty feet.

"Up with you," she called lightly and took hold of Francine's two hands. "I think a nice jaunt into the village would do us some good."

"Would it?" returned Francine doubtfully as she allowed Venetia to urge her to her feet. She pulled her pretty blue muslin into shape around her lean figure and asked, "Isn't the village very far away?"

"Not at all. No more than two miles. The exercise is just what we need, and we can stop in at the village tearoom for a bit of luncheon. Come on, Francie, believe me, it will be fun."

A biddable girl, Francine brightened. "All right. I'll just go fetch our cloaks, then, and meet you in the great hall."

"Right, and I will tell Bess we won't be in for lunch." However, she was caught up short when Francine stopped abruptly in the doorway, went rigid and backed into her.

"Venetia . . . oh no . . . Venetia . . ." cried Francine in some distress.

"What is it Francie? What . . ."

Francine spun around and took Venetia's arms in a tight grip.

"Taylor . . . my cousin . . . he is in the great hall . . . *he is here!*"

Chapter Three

Venetia's fine brow went up. "Well, to own a truth, I half expected him to arrive two days ago with you." She sighed with resignation. "I suppose that puts an end to our plans."

"No, oh no, now more than ever we must go out!" declared Francine.

"Why, Miss Fenton?" mocked Venetia quizzingly. "Don't you like your cousin?"

Miss Fenton considered this. "Oh? As to that, I suppose he is nice enough. It is just that ... I particularly want to ... avoid him."

"I don't understand," said Venetia reasonably.

"You see ... I didn't know he would be here. Grandmama said nothing about it ... and ... and I told George that Taylor would not be here!" wailed Miss Fenton distressfully.

"George? Who the deuce is George?" returned Venetia in some surprise.

There was no time for a reply, for at that moment Groomsby opened the drawing-room door and announced grandly, "Lord Westbourne."

Taylor came through the doorway and pulled up short to find two ladies near its threshold. The first of these two he knew well enough for his cousin, Francine, and he smiled as he took up her proffered hand. During this time, Venetia had time enough to take his full measure, and she discovered that once again he set her pulse to racing.

Perhaps it was the romantic manner his dark curls had of adorning his forehead? Perhaps it was the glow of his gray eyes? Then again, his shoulders, wide and without the fashionable support of wadding—they did his brown velvet cutaway coat justice enough to draw a lady's stare. She chided her fluttering heart. Wasn't he the same rude and haughty roué who had ignored her when he had been at Ingram Place three years ago? Yes, he was! Arrogance and self-assurance were written all over his marvelous form. He knew he was a fine figure of male masculinity. Conceited, that was what he was, and Venetia lifted her chin against his unconscious wiles.

Lord Westbourne's gray eyes turned and found a tall, lithe goddess of a woman whose white-gold cornsilk waves reached her neat waist, and he held himself in check. A beauty indeed, but never mind, look at her! Why, her eyes were sparkling green emeralds . . . but cold. No doubt, she had heard he was a . . . a *poor relation,* and like all her kind, held herself aloof. Vaguely he recalled having seen something of her three years ago. Three years ago, but then he had been going through hell and had really seen nothing.

"Enchanted, Miss . . .?" He bent over her hand, and damned if he could remember her name. He gently urged her to supply it.

She held it back, if only to make him uncomfortable. She knew nothing of the circumstances he had suffered three years ago. She only knew he had ignored her then. "Very good, my lord," she taunted, her green eyes ablaze. "Miss. That is an excellent start."

He grinned sheepishly. So the kitten had sharp claws. "I am sorry, and can't think how . . ."

She saved him. "Miss Tay, my lord. Venetia Tay." She moved away from him, as he still held her delicate hand.

He frowned. The chit clearly disliked him. Well, well, even in the wilds of Northumberland, the females held a man of little means at bay. He looked her over openly. It might be interesting to play with such game . . . hint at his newly acquired wealth. No, better sport the way it was.

Groomsby reappeared with the information that the squire was ready to receive his nephew, and Taylor made his bow to the women,

"Until later," he said softly, smiling wide at his cousin and quizzingly at Miss Tay.

When he was gone, Venetia spun around on Francine, and a low, fierce sound escaped her. "Oooh . . . what an odious man he is!"

"Who?" returned Francine in some surprise.

"Your miserable cousin!" snapped Venetia, and then quickly, "Oh, I am sorry . . ."

"Well, I don't think he is odious . . . though he can be terribly vexing at times, especially when he flirts outrageously with me, for it sends George into the boughs, and—"

"And that is another thing," interrupted Venetia. "*Who* is George?"

Francine blushed. "Oh," she said vaguely, "no one, really."

"No one really?" retorted Venetia on an incredulous laugh. "But if you don't want to tell me, I understand perfectly."

Francine reached out and touched Venetia's hand immediately. "It isn't that. Oh, Venetia . . . I am in such a tangle."

"Are you, love? Because of this George nobody?"

Francine giggled. "Silly . . . he isn't a nobody. In fact, he is the best of good ton . . . but hasn't a fortune, you see."

"Oh, and therefore he does not meet with Grandmama's approval," summed up Venetia neatly.

"That's it!" exclaimed Francine, pleased with Venetia's ready understanding.

Squire Ingram sat up in bed, his nightcap askew on his steel-gray wisps of hair, his vague, watery blue eyes darting around as he ordered his man to remove his tray from his lap. He was thin, sharp-boned, and had the aura of ill health hanging about his head, yet, even so, he was clear-headed and strong-willed.

Lord Westbourne was quick to note this as he

entered the room and received his initial shock, for his uncle's failing health had certainly told upon his person in the last three years.

"Uncle ..." said Westbourne, going forward and taking up Ingram's hand and giving it an affectionate squeeze.

"Don't think you can play off your tricks on me, upstart. It won't fadge."

"Won't it? I shall give up all attempts at cordiality, then." Westbourne laughed. "You relieve me. I was sure that turning you up sweet would pall on me."

"Stubble it!" retorted the squire (though very much amused by this his favorite relation). "I brought you here for a reason."

"Ah," said Westbourne, low and long for emphasis.

The squire eyed him ruefully. "Always so damned impudent! Mind, now ... you have quite a lot at stake here."

Westbourne bowed his handsome head. "So I do. How undutiful of me to forget it."

The squire screwed up his mouth and narrowed his eyes as he gazed at his nephew. "Sit down, Taylor."

Westbourne did as he was told and folded his large, well-made hands in his lap. "I am, as you see, Uncle, quite at your disposal."

Oddly enough it was at this juncture that the squire drew a long, sad sigh. It was a wistful sound and betrayed the fact that in spite of his harsh facade, there was a heart that felt.

"She was a good woman, my Gussie ... never meant to outlive the old gal." He shook his head. "Bah! No sense bleating on that. The fact is, I did outlive her. So what's to be done? Would have left m'fortune to her, you know . . . let her decide how to divide it up," he went off suddenly, found another realm and fancied himself a part of it. Then, just as quickly, he was back, staring hard at his nephew. "Well, well . . . wondering how I mean to divide up m'money, are you?"

"As a matter of fact, not in the least," said his nephew sweetly.

"Sauce-box!"

Westbourne hung his head dutifully. "Forgive me," he said, curbing his grin.

"Eh? What do you take me for . . . a damn flat? Don't play off your gammon with me!"

"I wouldn't dream of it, Uncle."

His uncle eyed him suspiciously but chose to continue. "The thing is, there is Venetia . . ."

"Venetia?" Westbourne's gray eyes flickered. "Ah, yes, Miss Tay."

"That's right. Not blood kin, you know . . . but I have always liked that spitfire! Looks like an angel, but pluck to the backbone, that girl, with never a mind to m'pockets."

"I see," said Westbourne, thinking that he did. His dry tone was not lost on his uncle.

The squire released a short, derisive laugh. "Think she has been cutting in on your time here, eh? Well, yes, so did I, at first"—he waved this consideration away—"but never mind that. Have it all settled."

"Have you, Uncle?" The quizzical look Westbourne cast his uncle was not unaffectionate, nor was it lost on the squire.

"Have a care, my buck, I'm not bacon-brained

and have a mind to cut you out of m'plans just for playing the fool with me. We both know I've come up with a solution. Now, do you want to hear, or don't you?" snapped the squire.

"I should like nothing better," said Lord Westbourne meekly.

His uncle knew better than to be deceived by this, but chose to continue. "There is Charles, more flash than foolish . . . don't like him above half, but he is your cousin and has as much Ingram blood in him as you do." With this the squire directed a look at his nephew's countenance. He grunted in dissatisfaction and proceeded, "And there is Francine, you know. A pretty little widgeon with not the least iota of sense." His voice was beginning to drag heavily, and he shook his head. "And there is Venetia."

"There is also Mr. Tay. I seem to recall that your . . . er . . . Venetia had a younger brother?" put in Westbourne curiously.

"He don't signify," returned the squire impatiently. "The lad inherits a small parcel when he turns five and twenty. Not concerned with him." He wagged an admonishing finger. "Now hold your tongue and let me finish." But his eyelids were already beginning to sag.

Westbourne saw that his uncle was looking seriously fagged and inclined his head with some concern. "If you feel you must, but really, Uncle, I think you should leave it till later."

"Blister it!" the squire managed to expostulate. "Now, where was I? I know, the three of you and Venetia. Have it all worked out . . ." He took a long drag of air and his head fell to one side. A moment later he was smacking his lips and his eyes were closed. He had fallen asleep.

Westbourne's features drew together and a sad sigh escaped as he pulled the covers round his uncle's frail form. Quietly he left the room and advised his uncle's man that the squire was sleeping. Now, this was all very interesting. So, Charles had been summoned as well, eh? Charles? The thought of his cousin drew a marring sneer to his sensuous lips. They traveled in different sets, had different principles and had too often engaged in warlike stances while at school and then later as young men taking on the *beau monde* to which they belonged. Now just what did his uncle have in mind? He didn't mean to divide up his estates— oh no, of that Westbourne was certain. It was too simple, and if Westbourne knew anything of his uncle, he knew the squire was playing a deep game!

Chapter Four

Charles MacGregor, Lord Iverness, stepped off the stage. His valet, Mulby, hurried at his back to gather the meager luggage they had brought and came up breathlessly to advise his employer that he had found a conveyance of sorts to take them the distance to Ingram Place.

Iverness looked about the quaint village and sighed. He had sustained a disheartening journey surrounded by those he felt were vastly beneath him on the social scale. Bitterly he had contemplated the injustice of fate, and now, now he looked up to discover the vehicle his man had found was nothing better than an ordinary gig, with a cob at its head. He stifled a groan and thanked his man.

"Ah, Mulby . . . what would I do without you?"

"Dinna ye think on it, m'laird; a guid dog ne'er barks aboot a bone."

His lordship released a short laugh and touched his diminutive servant's shoulder. "You may not be looking for a reward, Mulby, but I promise you, when I am in a position to do so, I shall repay you for your loyalty."

The driver of the weathered gig took them the distance in silence, and Charles MacGregor was able to take stock of his uncle's rich lands. He sat rigidly, for it was an embarrassment to find himself in such a position, but the last two years had been a tiresome drain on his pockets. The one thing that assuaged his humbled pride was that one day very soon, all this marvelous farmland, all his uncle's holdings, would be his. Then he would never be reduced to such penury again!

Ingram Place met the eye in sweeping boldness. Its neat park, its rolling lawns, the River Tweed that etched a path around its borders, all assailed the visitor with a demand to be appreciated. Lord Iverness scanned his surroundings and felt a wave of irritation. To think an English squire had managed to maintain all this, when his own Scottish home was crumbling. It was a source of exquisite pain, but never mind, he meant to make all right in the end!

The sixteenth-century house came into view, and it wasn't long before Groomsby was opening wide the front doors and sending a footman out to help Mulby with his lordship's portmanteau. If the Ingram butler was surprised at the vehicle Lord Iverness had hired, he hid it well and greeted the squire's nephew with placid politeness.

"Perhaps, my lord, you might wish to join your cousin and Miss Tay in the drawing room?" inquired Groomsby as he sent the footman with Mulby to the bedchamber prepared for his lordship's arrival.

"My cousin?" Iverness frowned. "Never say Westbourne is here?" This was a possibility that had slipped his mind.

The butler's brow itched to move, but he kept it in place, "Yes, my lord, though he is at present closeted with the squire. However, I meant your cousin Miss Francine Fenton."

"Francine? Good God! Are we then all gathered?" He was taken off guard with this information. "Who else might be coming?"

"I believe, my lord, that you are the last arrival."

"I see. And who did you say was with my cousin?"

"Miss Tay. Mrs. Ingram's niece." Groomsby frowned but decided to offer his lordship the information. "I believe she was away with Mrs. Ingram during your last visit to Ingram Place."

That was two years ago. Ah yes, he remembered the squire's mentioning the Tays. Well, they didn't matter, at least. "Well then, I suppose I shall first pay my respects to my cousin, Miss Fenton." He cast Groomsby a considering look. "I fancy I remember the way, but if you will in the meantime have a bath drawn for me in my chamber . . ."

"Very good, my lord," answered Groomsby, bowing respectfully. What he thought of Iverness was very carefully concealed.

The drawing-room door opened once again and Venetia found herself appraising a tall, angular, modestly (though fashionably) dressed Scotsman.

His mien was proud, his eyes hazel and strangely intent. His age she put at thirtyish, and his address she found boldly intriguing. She watched him as he came forward and took up Francine's delicate hand.

"Cousin . . . I can see that you are well, for you look enchanting," he said easily, his smile wide and, Venetia felt, not quite sincere. He turned and took her full measure, which immediately teased a twinkle into her eyes.

"Miss Tay . . . but ho, I needn't be so formal. We are connected, are we not?"

"In a manner of speaking," she said easily.

"Venetia, this is my cousin, Lord Iverness," started Francine in some confusion.

"Venetia!" ejaculated his lordship quickly. "What a lovely name." He was bending over her hand, his hazel eyes were coming up to discover with some pleasure that hers were green, bright and all too beautiful. "And you must call me Charles."

"Must I? We shall see," returned Venetia.

His eyes snapped guardedly. No fool here. What was this flaxen-haired beauty about? Was she after his uncle's fortune? What were her chances?

Venetia nearly read his thoughts, so clearly did they flit across his forehead, and she found herself cynically amused. She moved across to the sideboard and opened its glass-paned door.

"My lord, may I offer you some refreshment?"

"How kind," said Charles MacGregor, immediately making his way to her. "Please, do make yourself comfortable and allow me." His tone was polite, but clearly he would not permit her to play hostess in his uncle's house.

Venetia inclined her head and strayed nearer to the fire. Things were certainly moving along swiftly and not too comfortably. Francine broke the sudden silence.

"Charles . . . I don't understand. Did uncle send for you too?"

"It would appear that he did," he answered softly and took a long draft on his port.

"This is dreadful," breathed Francine in some distress.

Charles looked at her ruefully. "I agree," he said dryly.

Venetia was just a bit shocked. "It is not so unusual that your uncle should want you all near when he is so ill . . .?"

Charles studied her thoughtfully and toasted her silently with his glass. Francine put in on a worried note that Venetia did not understand.

"Don't I? Well, shall we leave your cousin to rest after his long journey and take that walk we planned?" Venetia meant to get to the bottom of Francine's agitation.

Once more this was put off by Westbourne's reappearance on the scene. He came in slowly, for his thoughts were busy and his concern over his uncle's state of health quite sincere. The vision of his cousin, Charles, leaning against the shoulder of a rich brown velvet Queen Anne chair brought him up short.

"I was wondering when you would arrive," said Westbourne dryly.

"You knew, of course, that I would," returned Charles MacGregor.

Westbourne inclined his head. "Of course."

"Ah, and I am as equally pleased to see you, cuz," returned Charles.

Francine did not notice this interchange, though Venetia took it all in, and therefore it was with some surprise that Francine captured Venetia's attention.

"Taylor . . . when you left London, did you see . . . well . . . did George know that you were on your way here?" asked Francine suddenly.

Westbourne tore his sardonic glance away from Charles and smiled wickedly at Francine. "Why no, my lovely."

She breathed a sigh of relief. "Thank goodness."

"Ah, but then I did not see him in London, so hasty was my departure. I did, however, find him in Nottingham."

"What?" shrieked Francine.

"I stopped over for a day to visit with some very old friends and was pleased enough to find George there . . . repining your absence from London." There was a decided twinkle in his gray eyes.

"Oh . . . oh dear . . ." breathed Francine, a blush stealing to her cheeks.

"That's right. So I rather thought he would be pleased to know that I was on my way to Ingram Place. I promised him I would look after you."

"You beast! You never did!" returned Francine in some irritation of nerves. "What did he say?"

"Odd, that. I had the very distinct feeling that if we were not such close friends I might have found myself called out."

"I won't have it, Taylor! Everyone knows you are a nonesuch with a pistol! You must not let him call you out."

"Nonsense. I would delope—I promise you." Westbourne laughed.

"Yes, but George might be so angry, he would not, and it would end in his killing you and having to flee the country, and I don't want him to have to flee the country!"

"No, that would never do," said Westbourne. "He is among your most ardent suitors, is he not?"

She turned to Venetia. "Please, Van . . . do let us take that walk now, for I find my cousin's company too provoking to endure!"

Venetia repressed her smile, for she had never seen Francine so worked up. She turned and made her leave lightly before following her friend out of the room. This was turning out to be far more interesting than she had anticipated!

Charles and Taylor were left to eye one another, which is exactly what they did. It was Westbourne who released a short, hard laugh. "Egad, Charles! Don't level your scowl at me! I had nothing to do with Uncle's plans."

"Didn't you? You have always been a favorite of his. But no, I don't suppose you would have prodded him to include me in his invitation. Francine, however? You have always had a *tendre* for our fair cousin."

"Have I? She is a sweet child. It would be strangely unnatural if I did not."

"Hmmm," thought Charles out loud. "And what of the beautiful Miss Tay? What does Uncle plan in her regard?"

Westbourne frowned. "That is something only Uncle knows at the moment."

"Really?" retorted Iverness on a snort. "I was under the impression that you were just above-stairs, visiting with the squire."

"So I was," said Westbourne glibly, adding nothing toward the conversation and moving off to the long window which overlooked the rolling lawns of the park.

"Ah . . . I see matters between us have not changed," said Charles quietly.

Groomsby entered the drawing room at that moment and bowed respectfully. "My lord," he said to Iverness, "I am told your bath awaits your pleasure."

"Thank you." Iverness nodded and began to follow Groomsby out of the room. He stopped at the doorway and said softly, "Cousin, I have a great deal at stake here and shan't be put off easily. Concerns at Ingram Place stand differently than they did in London, depend upon it!"

Westbourne watched the door close at his cousin's back. Indeed, matters at Ingram Place were dangerously different, and this time, unlike his last encounter with Charles, he did not feel the reins were in his own hands!

Chapter Five

Venetia slipped on her plain but serviceable blue wool night wrapper and quietly padded across her bedroom. A quick peek into the dark hall told her that the servants had snuffed all the wall sconces and were probably abed. Her long white-gold hair trailed at her back as she sped down the hall, cupping her candle as she went to safeguard its light. Again she made her way to her brother's bedchamber and knocked softly. Nothing. She knocked again, this time opening his door a crack. Still nothing.

"Gilly?" she called in a low voice. She put up her candle to discover that Gilbert Tay had still not returned home. "Deuce take it, Gilly," she said on a quiet but exasperated note, "just where are you?" She stood for a moment, closed his door and with a sense of purpose hurried down the hall to the backstairs. They creaked loudly as she took them, but never mind, with any luck Groomsby and Cook would be asleep? She put down her candle on a small square wall table and went to the rear door. Just as she thought. Groomsby had left it unbolted. He was fully aware that Gilly had not returned home and he was giving him a way into the house! With a determined arch of her fine dark brow, she slid the lever into place and folded her arms. "Well, Mr. Tay, when you come in, it will be through the front door, and guess who will be there to greet you!"

She took up her candle, and off she went again, down the narrow corridor which opened up at length to the central hall. The front door she found heavily bolted. These levers she undid, and with a soft smile she turned to the nearby library and went within. From the library she would hear the front door open, and then she would demand her brother join her in the library and explain. After all, this was beyond everything irresponsible. It was past twelve o'clock already. What a perfectly odious day it had turned out to be, what with Westbourne's arrival, and then Iverness's.

Dinner? Egad but that had been an awkward event. Iverness and Westbourne sparred throughout the meal, with Francine sullen and pettish. Gilly had not been in to meet with either Westbourne or Iverness on their arrival. And then Gilly's message had arrived advising her not to expect him for dinner. No explanation was offered in his terse epistle, and Venetia had worried about just what he was doing. Yes, she told herself, he was nearly of age ... a man, no doubt after a man's evening of pleasure. And yet, something deep-rooted in her knowledge of him told her that such things were not at the heart of his absence this evening!

Well, she meant to await his return in the quiet of the library, where she would be certain to hear his entrance into the hall. She opened the library door and went within to discover with something of surprise that the fire still burned brightly. They had retired after dinner to the library, where they had made a frugal attempt at conversation and cards. A dying fire was what she expected, not this blaze. Her lovely brow went up. The fire's light was a full glow, but the recesses of the cozy room were shrouded in darkness. She sighed, put her candle holder down and moved to a side table where she had put down her latest volume of Jane Austen. This taken up, she had started toward the winged chair flanking the fireplace when a voice, male and familiar, said softly at her back:

"Ah, Miss Tay, I see that I am not the only one after some ... er ... midnight amusement." Westbourne stepped out of the dark and came toward her. She spun around, and her hair of white-gold flew round her shoulders, her green eyes opened wide. He was struck with her beauty. Damn but she was a diamond ... and there was a mystery around her as well. He saw a guilty look shadow her countenance. Well, well, she was here for more than a book, but what?

Venetia had turned sharply to find him towering above her. Her heart took on an extra beat. What was he doing here? He was fully dressed. In fact, from the look of his windblown black hair and the sparkle to his eyes, she rather guessed he had just come in a little while ago. Well, that explained the fire. He must have been the one to put another log on. "Faith, my lord, you did startle me," she said reproachfully and then cocked her head on a playful note, for she could just faintly detect the aroma of ale about him. "I may be after a book to put me to sleep . . . but it seems to me you have had enough . . . er . . . activity to help you along to bed."

He laughed. "That's right. I mustn't forget you have a brother and know just how a restless male tires himself out." His tone was light, flirtatious, and he was moving closer to her. "As a matter of fact, I went into the village, to your local tavern there, and found the entertainment sadly lacking. Decided to be good, came home in search of Pope's essays"—his hand had found her waist and in one quick movement drew her near—"and found you instead." It was a whisper, and then suddenly, passionately, his mouth had her own.

What was happening? So quickly she didn't think, couldn't react. She was in his arms and he was kissing her. She was three and twenty and he was an experienced man who knew just how to melt a woman's will. She was shocked at herself, and it served to bring her to her senses. She yanked out of his embrace and with some show of force swung her arm with its open hand. He caught her wrist and saved himself. "No, pretty Venetia . . . I stole a kiss . . . but I would gladly give it back," which he seemed intent on doing.

She stood away, her hand outstretched, and stamped her foot against his onslaught, "Stop it, my lord! You are in your cups, and so I may consider forgiving you ... if you take your book of Pope and leave me immediately!" She was no schoolgirl miss to be frightened, but she would instantly show him that she wasn't a maid to trifle with. Her blood was racing, her knees were crumbling, and her head, oh faith, it was spinning, but he didn't know that! No, and she wasn't about to let him see.

He brought himself up. Rebuffed. He hadn't been sure about Venetia's character. He had watched her handle Iverness during dinner, and he had rather thought she had flirted with his cousin outrageously. It had been obvious that she considered herself her own woman. So what, then, innocent or jade? He was more than just a trifle bemused. Had his condition prompted him to behave improperly to Venetia, or had she aroused him to the moment? Her fault or his? Never mind. He made her a low bow.

"Forgive me, Miss Tay, but to say that I am sorry would be an untruth. However, I will leave you in peace and in hopes that the morning will find you feeling more charitable toward me." He started off.

She picked up his forgotten volume of Alexander Pope. "My lord?" she called coyly, for she wouldn't have him thinking her a missish frightened country girl. "You've neglected to take what you came for." He turned and she flipped the book toward him.

He caught it up with his two hands and tipped his head to it and her. "Have I, Miss Tay?" His meaning was clear, and his decision about her was: bold, saucy jade. She withheld with one purpose—to play, only to play.

Gilly moved within the stable aisle. He had only the moonlight filtering in from the stall windows and the barn door to guide him, but he knew his way about and had no difficulty finding the tackroom. He hefted his saddle onto its rack and hung up his bridle, moved off to the feed room and scooped up a quantity of fresh hay. He went back down the stone floor to his horse's box stall and answered his steed's gruff grunts for food.

"There now, Brutus, eat your hay and get some rest. We've had a long night." He checked his horse's water supply and then patted the dark bay's rump as he left.

The stables were put at his back as he scurried up the park lawns, shortcutting it to the house's rear door. With any good luck, Groomsby had left the door unbolted as usual. However, a hard tug at this portal disclosed the fact that this was not so. What had happened? Why was it locked? Damnation! What to do? He hurried around to the front door. Perhaps . . .? Gratefully, he found the door unbolted and slowly made his way within, turned and locked it before going on his toes and taking the dark central hall to the stairs.

"Poor Gilly . . . you must be tired," said a gentle voice in the darkness.

His heart jumped and he spun around. Half in relief and half with misgiving, for he recognized the danger in his sister's tone, he said, "Hang it, Van . . . you nearly scared the breath out of me."

"Oh, I rather doubt that, but . . ." She held the

library door open now so that he could see the inviting firelight. "Do join me. Why, it's been an age since I've seen you, and so much has happened that I should like to discuss with you."

Clearly there was no way of getting out of this. With some resignation, he crossed the hall to her side, mockingly bade her enter before him, which she did with an inclination of her head that sent a wary chill through him. She was angry, and he set himself ready for the inevitable.

She turned and eyed him. His face was dirtied with grease, and the clothes he wore were old and disheveled. One fine brow rose, and she reached out to touch his cheek. He pulled away, and she dropped her hand and said nothing about his appearance. Instead, very easily and brightly, she said, "Gilly, we have a houseful of people, and you were not here to see how the cousins get along with one another."

"Oh, Van . . . Van . . . I'm sorry. I quite forgot that Westbourne and Iverness were due. Have they been at you?" He looked genuinely concerned.

She relented. "No, dear . . . not at me, at one another. Westbourne and Iverness openly detest one another, and both are worthy opponents, let me tell you. But Francine . . ."

"Silly pea goose, that one, what has she been at? Setting Westbourne and Iverness at one another for her hand?"

"Why no . . . what makes you think she would do that?"

He shrugged. "Don't know that she would think of it on her own, but her grandmama no doubt told her she might inherit from Uncle. A title, you know, often makes the chits' heads swoon, and lo, she has two of 'em in the house!"

"Oh, Gilly, how can you be so . . . so cynical?" cried Venetia in some distress, for he was showing her a side she had never seen before.

"How can you be so naive? Wake up, Venetia! Don't you see what is going on around you?"

Venetia sighed. "What are you saying, that Westbourne and Iverness are here to inherit? Why shouldn't they be? Gilly, they are his heirs."

He shrugged. "That is not all the squire is up to, Venetia . . . and I want you ready—"

"Look, Gilly, you have turned the subject around nicely, but it won't fadge! You can't fob me off. I want to know where you have been and what you have been doing."

He pulled himself up. "That's half the trouble Van. Look at me. Do you think I'm still ten years old?"

"No, but . . ."

"But what? Just how old do you think I am?"

"Old enough to get into the worst kind of trouble," she answered promptly.

He scoffed at her. "I know better than to get caught." As these words slipped out he bit his lip. He was tired, and his tongue had rolled before he had been able to think.

"You ragamuffin! So you are up to mischief. Gilly . . ."

He touched her shoulder. "Leave it be, Van. I'm home now, see, safe and sound. I don't want to lie to you . . . so don't pry at me any longer."

"But Gilly—" she started.

"Hush, girl. It's enough. Don't mother me."

"I'm not. It is just that I am worried. Don't you know . . ."

"Come on," he said, taking her hand and leading her to the door. "We both need some sleep if we are going to face the squire and his lineage in the morning."

Westbourne, finding himself summarily dismissed some moments before by Venetia, left the library and discovered the nether regions of the house. There he found the kitchen larder, and happily he discovered the squire's meanness did not extend to the cheese bin. There he helped himself to a generous portion, sliced it up with an apple and sat munching peacefully. While he devoured his midnight snack he allowed himself to dwell on the facts at hand.

Venetia. Beautiful. Yes, no denying that. A jade? Very possibly. She was a poor relation, yet her wardrobe indicated that her wiles had been used to induce the squire to spend lavishly on her. Uh-huh! Proof indeed of her power over his uncle. Unmarried. Yes, that was an odd thing indeed. How was it that she was three and twenty and still not married?

There was Francine. Did Francine mean to increase her dowry and return to London to marry the duke? Good Lord . . . he hoped not. And what of Iverness? Would he take his inheritance and return to Scotland, or would he be off for London again? This was not a thrilling thought, and with something of a sigh he got to his feet and started down the long narrow hall toward the main staircase. With mild interest he heard the sound of voices in the library, and his pace slowed. As the library door opened, he stopped completely and held himself in check in the darkness of the hall, snuffing out his candle and keeping out of view.

Gilly's voice came, soft and yet resolute. "Listen to me, Van, you deserve more and I mean to see you get it!"

"Gilly, do you know, that sounds more like a threat than a promise, and mark me, lad, if you don't take care, I shall marry my vicar and thwart all your great plans!" Venetia retorted. "I am a good deal out of patience with you!"

He laughed shortly, lightly. "I know better than that, m'girl! You would no more marry the good vicar than you would Westbourne!"

As brother and sister continued their quiet argument up the stairs and out of earshot, Westbourne felt a sense of pique. What the devil did they mean, comparing him to some unknown vicar, and why the deuce wouldn't she think of marrying him? Oh, of course, like the good vicar, he was thought to be penniless! Another female, formed like all her kind, to chase after the full-pocketed man!

Chapter Six

The morning was clear, crisp and promising. It was early yet, and the squire's relatives would not be down for breakfast for some time, Venetia reasoned as she went through the files of blossoming mums and cut long stems for her basket. She was a fetching sight with her long bright hair gathered in a tight bun at the top of her shapely head. She wore a rich brown morning gown of cambric that was long-sleeved, high-necked and high-waisted. Its wide scalloped collar and sleeve cuffs were made of ivory lace, and Ferdy thought her angelic as he caught up her hand and stopped her from snipping at another bloom.

"Venetia ... look at me ... it is the least a fellow deserves when he is proposing marriage!"

She eyed the young man seriously. "Don't be nonsensical. Ferdy, one day you will thank me—"

He cut her off, his tone desperate. "Thank you . . . for breaking my poor heart?"

She touched his cheek, and he held her hand fervently. "I'm not breaking your heart, Ferdy . . . but expanding it."

He frowned. "Venetia . . . Venetia . . ." He sought refuge in her gloved fingers, taking them to his lips. "All my hopes are centered in you."

"Ferdy, I am older than you," she said, trying logic.

He snapped it away in the air. "What are two years or so? What do they mean to people in love?"

She tried reason. "But Ferdy"—gently, to spare his feelings—"I am not presently in love."

He clasped both her hands, and her basket of flowers dropped unheeded to the grass. "Not in love? Well, of course you are not, how could you be, here, with the walls of Ingram Place closing in on you?"

Venetia wanted to point out that this was reason enough for most maids to run headlong into their first savior's arms, but she allowed him his moment.

"Venetia . . . listen to me. I will take you away, to London, as my bride. I will give you the world. You will end in adoring me. It will be perfect . . . you are perfect . . ."

She pulled out of his hold, for she could see Groomsby rushing at them, and he had the look of a harried man, "Ferdy . . . I think Groomsby wants our attention."

"Hang Groomsby!" retorted Ferdy, but he did allow his hands to drop to his side and he did pull himself up to his full height, noting with something of a darkling expression that he fell some inches shorter than the good butler.

"Miss Venetia," started Groomsby on a breathless note, "I am so glad I've found you. The squire has been working himself into a frenzy. He has called all his relatives to his bedside—even your brother is with him—and he is shouting after you."

Venetia's hand went to her cherry lips. "Oh no ... Groomsby, is he ... is he ...?"

Groomsby shook his head. "Oh no ... as to that, he seems no worse than he was yesterday. No, he wants an audience for something he has to say, and he won't say it until you are part of that audience."

Venetia turned to Ferdy, saw his distressed expression, and in a sisterly fashion dropped a light kiss upon his cheek. "Later, Ferdy ..."

Westbourne had been standing by the window in his uncle's bedchamber, and from that long, wide glass he could see the rows and rows of brightly colored mums; he could also see Venetia and Ferdy. His dark brow went up to see Ferdy pressing her hand, kissing her gloved fingers. Thoughtfully he watched them as his uncle ranted at his back regarding Venetia's absence.

Damn, but look at her kissing that puppy! One could not really blame her—stuck up here in the wilds, he supposed she didn't have much selection—and still, this was cradle-robbing indeed! A quick fluttering went through him when he thought of her in his arms, and he chided it away. She was just another clawing beauty, nothing more.

"What are you finding so interesting out there?" demanded the squire petulantly.

"The River Tweed, Uncle. I never realized before how closely it cuts your property," returned Westbourne easily.

"Eh? Taking stock, are you?" The squire cackled over this for a moment and then bit into a biscuit. It crumbled all over his nightshirt, but he didn't bother to brush it away.

Quietly, unhurriedly, Venetia entered the room. "Squire, I understand you have been wanting me?" She turned to the assembled company. "Good morning, everyone." She went to Gilly, and because he was looking out of temper and sour she placed a kiss upon his forehead, going on her toes to do the job.

Westbourne was drawn to her, found her graceful, elegant and very much a lady. Here was an intriguing piece indeed, he thought absently and took a backseat to the party.

The squire's complexion was gray, and Venetia could see that while Groomsby was correct in saying her uncle was no worse, neither was he any better. She went to him and patted his hand, for he was grumbling about her lateness on the scene. "Well, I am here now, squire." Her green eyes teased.

"So you are, sauce-box, so you are," the squire answered. His eyes strayed and found Gilly's expression. "Don't you be scowling at me, lad! In the end you may come to see that I've done what is best!" He fell into coughs, and it was Venetia who thought to pour out a glass of water and hand it to him. He took it up, swallowed and sighed. "Aye . . ."

His eyes were keen again, bright with the mischief he contemplated. To Venetia he said in a low voice, "You've never given a fig for my money—never haggled after it—and I'd swear you've never liked me."

"Sometimes, squire, we care for someone . . . even though we find we don't approve of him," she answered, and her green eyes twinkled affection.

Westbourne silently drew in breath. Well, was it any wonder that his uncle had been taken in by such a chit? Egad, but she had a way of using her eyes. Vividly he recalled his own unforgivable behavior the evening before and the touch of her lips. . . .

"Aye, lass, you've done right by me. I'm not denying that, and what's more, you've earned your keep here, but still, that don't entitle you to have what should go to m'own blood heirs!" His tone dismissed her with its curtness.

Venetia wanted to answer, put him down sharply, but he was an old sick man, and she let it go. Her long dark lashes brushed her cheek as she controlled herself, and when those lashes lifted it was to find Westbourne looking full into her face. She blushed. She couldn't say why, or perhaps it had something to do with the memory of their encounter the previous evening. All too warmly the image of his face, the dark, intense expression of his eyes, came back to her. She found his face now, his eyes now, and he winked at her audaciously. Why, how dare he! Sharply she looked away and could almost feel him silently laughing at her.

The squire scanned Francine and clucked. She

was standing by the window looking out on the park lawns, absently perusing the loveliness of the autumn day.

"Silly goose!" complained Ingram. "You looking at the Tweed too? Well, I didn't call you in here to my bedside to daydream!"

Francine spun around and flushed. "Oh, excuse me, Uncle." She went forward.

Iverness said beneath his breath as she passed, "So solicitous, Francine. Excellent." Clearly his tone was derisive and threw her into greater confusion.

"You are horrid!" she snapped at him.

"Eh, what's this?" asked the squire with some intensity. "You children at one another?" This he found exquisitely funny, and his laughter sent him into a convulsion of coughing.

Again, it was Venetia who handled him gently, propped up his pillow, told him with something of a challenge in her tone that they might never hear what he had brought them to listen to if he continued in this vein.

He looked up into her face with a quiet admiration, and his voice was very low. "You've never been mealy-mouthed like most of your kind, have you? No, not you . . . though a fortune may be dependent upon it. Well, well, perhaps it has served you after all."

Both Iverness and Westbourne heard this clearly enough, and Westbourne felt a sneer pull at his mouth. So, it was exactly as he had thought. The beauty, Venetia, had worked herself into the squire's favors. He was sipping black coffee in a leisurely fashion; as she moved away from the bed, he raised his cup to her and was only a little surprised to see her blush.

"Squire . . . may I suggest that we leave you to rest? Perhaps another time might prove—" started Ivernes.

"Stubble it! I mean to tell you all now why I brought you to Iverness." He looked at Gilly. "No, you ain't dismissed, lad. This directly concerns your sister."

Gilly pulled himself up and eyed his uncle. There was no affection there. "I am fully aware of that, squire, and had no intentions of leaving."

The squire's brow went up, but he said nothing to this. Westbourne found himself liking young Tay, and after a moment said quietly to draw attention away from the lad, who was blushing furiously over his stand, "Uncle, perhaps, if you feel up to it that is"—a clear challenge—"you might find it timely to advise us now why we are all here."

The squire's fulminating eyes turned on Westbourne and softened.

"Eh . . . yes, yes, and by God, I do feel up to it, for I have been looking forward to watching your faces." He took a long breath. "I've made out a new will, you see." He frowned. "Gussie was my heir . . . but she was ever a scatterbrain. Had no business dying before me . . . but never mind, she did, so I had to figure out what I was to do with my money." He looked up at that and smiled at Westbourne. "If I were to be guided by inclination, I'd leave it all to you, Taylor. You are a man after m'heart . . . though from the tales I hear about your activities, you need curbing. Well, well, so I hit upon this plan to settle all of you comfortably . . . and I mean to be in on it at its start."

"Here it comes," whispered Gilly to his sister. "Maybe you should sit down."

"Hush," she said softly and touched his arm.

Westbourne watched brother and sister. Why he should was a question that did not at that moment occur to him, but he found himself interested and then intrigued by their behavior.

"There you are . . . blood relatives . . . Iverness, a great lord in Scotland but without a sou to his name . . . you there, Taylor, a lord in London with your family's estate home in mortgage and your affairs not much better than Iverness's." He shook his head. "You could split it down the middle . . . but what of Francine? Three ways? What of Gussie's Venetia? Tay there is provided for when he turns twenty-five . . . but Venetia now, she has no dowry. Gussie always wanted Venetia established . . . settled off . . . must do it for Gussie's sake," he said gruffly and then looked at Iverness. "Ho! Now if I wanted to split it four ways, I could, there is enough to make you all comfortable . . . but that's not what I wanted! So, I've decided on a double wedding!"

All at once Venetia saw. She took a step forward. "Squire . . . you can't mean it!" Her brother held her in check, and she turned on him. "Gilly . . . you knew?"

"No, I suspected. I understand his mind . . . I know you think I never have, but I do, Venetia, and I had a feeling, I just had a feeling," said Gilly.

Westbourne put his hand up to everyone, for they all looked about ready to talk at the same time. "Perhaps, Uncle, you might explain?"

"Eh? Thought I did . . . ah, the details, right then. Here are Francine and Venetia. Beauties . . . each in her own way. I've got m'own preference, so I've divided up the bounty in terms of sixty-forty. One of these chits gets more than the other, but only if they marry m'nephews."

"Hell and fire!" snapped Iverness before he knew what he was about. "You mean to marry us off . . . for money? Well, that may be, but what if these young ladies don't wish it? What then?"

"They will be throwing away a fortune," answered the squire.

"Hold!" said Venetia on an angry note. "This is beneath you, squire. It may be that Francine and I cannot be bought. Then what happens to your nephews and their inheritance?"

The squire eyed her thoughtfully. "I should worry about that if I were you."

"Oh! This is infamous," said Venetia in some distress. "You mean to disinherit your nephews if we don't accept your absurd terms?"

"I told you the terms of m'will," said the squire, waving her objection off. "I've got some time . . . maybe a week . . . maybe two; maybe only a day before I take the road to my maker. In the meantime, these lads had best decide which one of you they mean to wed and get to the business. I want to print the announcement in the *Gazette* before I lope off."

Francine had been listening to all this in stupefied shock. She turned now to Venetia and moved to touch her arm. "Van . . . what am I to do?"

Venetia patted her hand. "Come, Francine. We shall retire to the drawing room." She looked at her uncle rigidly. "We'll light a blazing fire and discuss this." And then in a grieved tone, "I had not expected such a trick from you. Perhaps Gilly has been right all along, and I have been blind." With this she turned and left the room.

Westbourne watched her go, watched Gilly rush to open the door for her and follow her out. All this was very astonishing, and because he was financially independent, laughable. However, he saw immediately that for someone in dire straits, it was a mean business, and he felt it in his heart to pity Iverness. He could announce his disinterest in the plan, announce the fact that he was a wealthy man and take himself out of the fray. Perhaps that would make his uncle leave the money, the estate, to Iverness. And then he saw his uncle's set expression. Nothing would move him. He wanted to hold the strings. Never mind, he could still leave. Then for mercy's sake, why wasn't he taking off? His uncle was dying . . . of course he must be near him at such a time. It was a good answer.

Iverness cleared his throat. "They don't appear to want us."

"You are both of you handsome men . . . you know how to turn a woman's head. You'll do it now. Francine will take one of you . . . her

Grandmama will see to that. And I've written to her telling her what I mean to do. She won't let a fortune slip through that child's hands. Francine is biddable . . . she will take one of you."

"I have noticed that Venetia is not . . . er . . . biddable," said Westbourne.

"Venetia biddable? Ha! Whoever gets that one gets a vixen," mused the squire out loud.

"But Uncle, will she, do you think, take one of us?" asked Charles thoughtfully, and to himself he added, And which one inherits the bulk of the estate?

"Venetia? I've been selfish, you know . . . kept her here with me. She'll end a spinster if she don't take one of you, for she won't have that prosing vicar of hers, and the other, that young'un Ferdy, would never do for her. No, he's a boy, she's a woman." He shook his head. "She won't like it, but she'll bend to my will, see if she won't." He heaved a long heavy sigh, and his lids drooped. "I'm tired now . . . go on . . . get out of here . . . and start your courting!" With this last, he chuckled, snorted and closed his eyes.

Out of the room, Iverness and Westbourne regarded one another, and it was Iverness who said softly, "Now which one do you think he means to have the sixty percent?"

Without hesitation and with something of a smirk Westbourne said, "Venetia."

"Precisely. I think I shall take our uncle's good advice, for 'courting' the fair Venetia may prove to be . . . enjoyable."

"And Francine?" prodded Westbourne.

"She has always been yours for the taking, hasn't she? No, I rather think Venetia will do for me."

"With my blessing," said Westbourne making his cousin a mock bow, but even so, there was an edge to his voice.

Chapter Seven

Venetia's reaction to the news was to explode. She had never had much rein over her temper. Into her room she stomped, leaving Francine to herself with an agitated "I can't discuss it any more, Francine . . . not now!" Slam went her door some moments later. Her eyes lit on a vase with wickedness in mind, but this urge she controlled, and in an attempt to steady herself, she crossed her arms over her middle and held them pressed against her. Did the squire really think he could manipulate her like this? A knock sounded at her door. " Yes?" she called.

"I am sorry to bother you, Miss Tay, but I wondered if I might have a word with you." It was Taylor.

She frowned to herself, for her heart, which was already beating far too rapidly, picked up its pace, and she found it hard to reply; she did at last go to the door and hold it open. Face to face they eyed one another for a long quiet moment. "What do you want, my lord? Surely you haven't come to propose already?"

He chuckled in spite of himself, for he was out of patience with her very fine acting. She had done this. Somehow she had thought of this notion and instilled the fancy in his uncle. It made no odds to him, because he could walk away . . . but what if he hadn't been able to? What if he weren't financially independent? "As a matter of fact, Miss Tay, I don't think I should propose to you. We wouldn't . . . er . . . suit."

She put up her chin. How dare he! Oooh! The unmitigated gall, the boor! "Excellent, for I am of the same opinion," she managed.

"I am, however, interested in your reaction to my uncle's demands."

"My reaction?" She was surprised and her green eyes opened wide.

He was impressed and inclined his head. "You do that so well, Miss Tay, a lesser man might think you in earnest."

She colored up with rage. "*Think* me in . . . why, you . . . get out of my doorway. This discussion has ended."

He was unmoved by her fury but again inclined his head. "Then you were not shocked by my uncle's mandate?"

"Shocked? Oh no, it is just the sort of thing he would do. Amazed that he should think *I* would go along with it, is a better description!" With this she started to close her door.

He put up his hand and stopped the door. "Do you mean for me to believe that you won't have my cousin?"

"Your cousin, my lord, has not yet proposed, but what I will or will not have is none of your concern!" She eyed his hand, and he allowed it to fall from the door. A moment later that edifice stood between them. Westbourne couldn't move for a long moment. She was certainly angry . . . or was that feigned? Perhaps she had expected to inherit a tidy sum and marry the country bumpkin of her choice? Perhaps that was at the root of her anger?

Venetia had been in a temper before his lordship's untimely visit. She was now in a blind fury. Off went her clothes and some of her buttons. This added to her agitation. She dove into her wardrobe and produced her brother's linen shirt and his country breeches. He had worn them some years ago, and they fit her to perfection. She shrugged on a tailored corduroy riding jacket, pulled on her weathered boots, and headed for the backstairs in the assembled trappings she wore when she intended hard riding.

When her Aunt Gussie had been alive, she had seen at once that her niece was an accomplished horsewoman. The squire kept prime livestock for pulling his coach and curricle, but in those days there hadn't been a mount in the stables for Venetia's daily use. So Aunt Gussie had taken up the cudgels in her sweet way, and she had not stopped until the squire had purchased Venetia a horse, a lovely chestnut that he had picked up at a country fair at a nominal cost. The filly had been four years old, spirited and green. It had taken Venetia nearly a year, and some bumps, bruises and interesting falls; it had taken even more perseverance, but in the end the mare proved her worth. Missy she was dubbed, and she was a source of great pleasure and comfort to Venetia. It was to Missy that she went whenever things became just too much to handle all at once. It was to Missy that she went now.

Ooooh! Her brain was seething. How could he? How dare he? Why did he? Westbourne was a cad! A rude and selfish boor! But why did he think she was some scheming, grabbing creature? What had put such a notion in his head? She wasn't any happier about the squire's will than he was! And oh, things did look bleak.

What to do? Marry the vicar and have done with these Ingram people! Gentle John, the vicar, would make her a good husband. Yes, and he would bore her to tears! Then Ferdy, for at least he was fun to be with. And a babe! Would she take such advantage? She had to do something. Soon the squire's house and all else would go to his family.

Devil take all these wilful, horrid men away! It made her want to cry. She didn't, though. That was not an answer, and an answer to her dilemma was what she needed. Things were quickly moving into disorder, but now, now she had to relax, and she needed Missy to do that.

The groom was busy enough with the mucking out of the stalls so he didn't raise an objection when she took up the lead and said that she would fetch Missy herself from the pasture. Some minutes later, her horse was cross-tied in the aisle and she was currying and brushing the mare's rich red coat. Thirty minutes passed before she was tacked up and leading her animal outdoors. Nimbly she mounted, quietly, easily she urged her horse forward, and off they went down the drive. The work had taken off the edge to Venetia's temper. Her soul? Her soul she was leaving to her horse!

George Whitney lived in an age when Lord Byron had unwittingly created the Byronic hero, a reckless being contemptuous of society, which described Mr. Whitney's character fairly accurately. He was tall, lean, with pronounced cheekbones, dark curly auburn hair always in disarray from a habit he had of attacking it whenever he was vexed, which was often and over almost anything. He was charming, he was wild-eyed and wild-tempered, he was unconventional about his clothing, which gave him the dashing air of a buccaneer. He was six and twenty and had his own set of rules, very many of them rather surprisingly prudish, but he was a popular figure in spite of his dangerous faults, and he was well liked by his peers. He was also in love. Desperately, tragically in love with Francine Fenton, and so he had been for the past four months.

Off she went, not making him any promises, to her uncle's in Northumberland, and he was desolate. However, she had assured him that Westbourne would not be there. He did not object to Westbourne. In fact, Taylor was one of his

closest friends. However, he did object to Westbourne's relation with Francine, which allowed
his lordship liberties he himself was not permit-
ted. There too, though Westbourne would laugh
off his objections, he could never be certain that
Taylor did not want Francine for himself. After
all, who could not want Francine? There was that
swine, the duke, who would propose the moment
she acquired Ingram's fortune!

Such disturbing thoughts sent him off to Nottingham, where he had friends willing enough to
amuse him out of his dismals. The next morning,
who should arrive to relieve his mind but Westbourne, and George felt well disposed toward his
old friend.

"You here, Taylor! Why, that is beyond everything great!" exclaimed George, shaking his
lordship's hand. "We'll go hunting tomorrow . . .
the dogs are all primed for the chase."

Westbourne had not planned on staying more
than the night, but the company was good and he
had joined the fox-hunting party the next morning. George had for a time forgotten his troubles,
and then betrayal most foul reared. "What? Off to
Ingram's?" returned George when Westbourne announced his destination.

"Well . . . er . . . yes," said Westbourne, at a
loss to understand his friend's sudden burst of
temper.

"You are not supposed to be going there!" snapped
George.

"No? How came you by such a decision?"

"By God!" cried George, beside himself, his hand
now running through his bright auburn curls,

"The girl has deceived me! What does she think me, a flat? Did she think I would not find out?"

An understanding look came into Westbourne's eyes, and he took pity. "George ... no doubt Francine had no idea I had been ... er ... commanded to Northumberland, like herself. We both know she is not capable of telling a deliberate lie."

He took a tour of the room and turned those wild, gleaming hazel eyes on Westbourne. "Yes, we both know that, don't we, Taylor! You mean to have her for yourself and will use every opportunity to arrange it!"

"And is that what you think? You believe I would advance myself while attending my uncle's sickbed? What a very poor opinion you have of me, George." Westbourne's mouth set in a hard line and his gray eyes grew coldly distant.

Contrarily and in some frenzy George waved this away. "If I thought that, Taylor, I would have already called you out!"

It took a moment, and then Westbourne's features relaxed. He went forward and touched his friend's arm. "Here ... if you fear the worst, join us in Northumberland and spar with me for the fair Francine's hand."

"Aha! Then you admit it! You are after her!" raged George.

"I admit nothing, old friend." He took up his hat. "Now I must bid our hostess and host adieu, for I'm off. And George, there is a lovely little inn situated between Ingram Place and the village of Cornhill on Tweed."

"Ha! What good would it do me!" shouted George,

off on one of his tantrums. "Go on, then . . . go
have at her. She won't take you!"

The devil in Westbourne returned, "Oh? Won't
she, George?"

It was these parting words that finally decided
George. True, his company at the Applegates' was
beginning to get trying, for he was in his worst of
moods, and they were heartily glad to see their
dear friend off. Thus he managed to find the
Boar's Head Inn on the River Tweed and to pro-
cure a room there at no very great cost. He had
come up with his riding mount in tow behind his
neat but small curricle. George Whitney came
from a long line of noble blood. True, he had not
inherited the title. That had gone to a cousin, as
did most of the Whitney fortune. However, he had
a comfortable, respectable living and was well
able to afford the necessities of life. He even felt
that he was able to afford Francine. However,
Francine's grandmama did not agree, and thus
George Whitney had been forbidden to Miss Fenton.
But Francine, like most young women, found
George a very romantic figure. It was as if the
dashing hero had stepped out of the pages of her
favorite novel. In addition to this, he was now
made unattainable, which made Francine yearn
for him all the more. However, she was, as was
stated earlier, a biddable child nearly always eager
to please the grandmother she felt she owed her
loyalty to.

His carriage, his horses and his belongings now
taken care of, George took his dark roan and
headed toward Ingram Place. His directions were
only fuzzy sentences in his mind, for he was rarely

able to heed such things. He would ask the question and scarcely listen to the reply, for his mind would already be elsewhere. So it was that in some exasperation he decided to ride up to a farmhouse and ascertain his location in relation to the squire's residence.

"Damn!" There was a four-foot fence in the way. He was an accomplished rider, but jumping fences was not something he did well, especially fences this high. He looked the length of the field and discovered that the fence made an attractive frame for it. "Well, old fellow," he said to his horse, "it's over we go." He put the roan into a canter and rushed his fence. It was his first mistake. He threw himself into position before his horse, which was his second mistake. His third and most deadly was that he angled the jump, which threw him off balance. Down went his toes, off went his calves, and over he went. He released a long worried yelp and landed with a thud on the soft turf.

Venetia's mood took her racing down the bridle path that circumvented the main pike. Here was a clear long run, and she took it with open reins. It was exhilarating, exciting and dangerous, and it did much to restore her to a sense of herself. She eased her horse gently, bringing the mare into a collected canter, and Missy objected by pushing her nose out and taking hold of the bit.

"Brat!" laughed Venetia as her horse kept up the heady pace, and then, less gently, she tugged on the reins, turning her young mare's head and managing to slow her a bit. The mare snorted, but accepted her mistress's decision. Soon they were approaching Farmer Perkens's field at a walk. It was a jump to attain the second field, for the good farmer discouraged riders from his land, but Venetia had it in mind to go up to the farmhouse and pass a space of time with Mrs. Perkens. She found the lowest portion of the long fence and cantered in line toward it. With her heels well down, her release well up on her mare's mane and her calves squeezing, she urged her horse over. It was like flying. It was a long and wonderful feeling, and as she landed she laughed brightly, but the laugh died abruptly as she saw a rider on the opposite side of the field take a bang-up fall!

Venetia galloped across the open, long-grassed field, pulled her horse up, jumped quickly off and went to George Whitney just as he was managing to sit up with a groan and a hand to his now uncovered and aching head. She noticed at once that even in his ruffled state he was rather good-looking in a gaunt and lean fashion. "Oh, sir . . . don't move for a moment. You have probably been winded."

George Whitney looked up and saw Venetia hazily before his swimming vision. In love with Francine he most certainly was, but he could not help but observe that the creature in boy's clothing had the loveliest of white-gold hair blowing around her very beautiful face. Green eyes scanned him with concern, and he felt it necessary to bring himself to order. "My . . . hat?" he said in an odd tone, for he was clearly embarrassed to be found in such a position and hoped to divert the girl while he got to his feet.

"Your hat?" returned Venetia at once, surprised.

"Of course," she said, turning about to look for the wayward thing. She discovered it in the tall grass, and as she fetched it, noticed out of the corner of her eye that he was getting to his feet. He swerved unsteadily and she ran to support him. His arm went around her and she found herself in close quarters with the stranger.

She was a neat bundle, taller than he was wont to appreciate, but a most delectable child. He needed something to get his mind off Francine's treacherous fickleness, and perhaps this rough-and-tumble creature would do. "My name," he said softly, "is George Whitney, and I find myself most grateful for your service."

Aha! He had taken her for some farmer's daughter, no doubt. Her clothes and the fact that she was unchaperoned. She smiled, not in the least offended. "Well, I am pleased to meet you, Mr. Whitney, and am only sorry for the circumstances. Look, are you well enough to ride? My uncle's home is not far from here, and you might rest there with some refreshment." Whitney, she thought quickly, George Whitney. Why did the name sound so familiar? She smiled to herself, for his thoughts flickered across his countenance so very clearly. He was astonished with her easy manners. She could see it and it amused her greatly.

"Your uncle?"

"Yes, Squire Ingram is—"

He cut her off and his tone was certainly fevered all at once. "Ingram? Ingram is your uncle?" he demanded.

"Yes," she said in what she hoped was a soothing voice, for he seemed far too excited over the fact.

"By God!" uttered the young man, "I have been searching for Ingram Place this hour and more. Never say it was just under my nose all this time?" He seemed disgusted with himself.

"Well, not precisely, but it is close enough." She released a little giggle. "And we won't have to take any fences flying, either . . . the farmer has a gate just north of here that will let us onto the main road. We can just cut across, and it will take us to Ingram property."

"God-sent is what you are! I have been all over the county looking for Ingram Place."

All at once Venetia's puzzled expression left her. "Why of course!" she exclaimed, well pleased with herself. She had an answer at last. "You are Francine's George Whitney!"

He pulled himself up, his mood once again blue. "Yes, that I have been from the first moment I clapped eyes on her, but whether Francine will ever be mine is quite another matter altogether."

"Oh, now don't pucker up, Mr. Whitney." Venetia laughed cheerily. "All is not quite lost. Very nearly, but not totally."

"What do you mean?" he asked hastily, picking up on this last with a vehement wildness in his hazel eyes.

"Well, don't bite my head off." She sighed. "I take it that you are . . . in love with Francine?"

He dropped his head a moment and then raised his gleaming eyes to say most dramatically that he was.

"Very well. Is Francine in love with you?"

"I thought for a time that she was not indifferent toward me," he said quietly.

"But her grandmama objects?" This was conjecture, for Francine had told her nothing about the affair.

"I am not titled and I am not rich," he said frankly.

"So her grandmama objects," she said, stating a case. "Are you, sir, able to support a wife?"

"Most certainly and quite comfortably," he returned, chin up and head wondering why he was answering this impudent girl's questions.

"Well then, we must do something about this sad state of affairs!" She went to her horse, who was grazing idly nearby. "Well, Mr. Whitney, come along. I will tell you how things stand as we ride."

George Whitney didn't even think to dissent from her command. He meekly followed her lead and for the next twenty minutes hung on every word. Oh, now and then he was unable to restrain an oath, especially when he heard the terms of Squire Ingram's will, but for this lapse he begged Venetia's pardon. Having sustained such lapses from her brother and his friends over the years, she found herself excusing him easily, and it wasn't long before the two discovered that they enjoyed one another's spirited company.

Chapter Eight

Their horses in the hands of the capable Ingram groom, Miss Tay and Mr. Whitney proceeded to the front door of the large manor house, where Mr. Whitney (ever wantonly displaying his flickering emotions) was moved to touch Miss Tay's gloved hand.

"So then, I may . . . count you an ally?" His hazel eyes were in grim earnest.

Venetia was not shocked or put off with the easy manner he had already adopted with her. She was in fact, quite pleased. However, she did withdraw her hand. Her smile made up for it,

"Yes, Mr. Whitney, I think you may. At least we are both agreed on one point: Francine should not be wasted on Lord Westbourne!"

"Capital!" exclaimed George just as Groomsby opened the door wide. That worthy's expression was not lost on the young people, and they immediately burst into ready mirth.

"Hello, Groomsby. This is Mr. George Whitney, here to pay us a visit." She turned to Mr. Whitney, who was looking about, evidently for Francine. "Say hello to Groomsby, George." She bit her lower lip, for his first name came all to readily to her lips.

George did not seem to notice this lapse in conduct. "Hello, Groomsby," he said quite cheerily and followed Venetia's steps down the long wide hall.

"I don't mean to cast a rub on your good humor my friend," whispered Venetia as Whitney caught up to her, "but there is that miserable will to contend with."

He snapped his fingers in the air. "To perdition with such frippery things. I am a man in love."

Venetia laughed as she opened the drawing-room door, "I can see that you are, but remember, my buck, we are not playing at ducks and drakes, you know."

All too near, far too gripping, Venetia heard a male voice that swung her head around.

"Are we not? I can't see why, for ducks and drakes, though a child's sport, does afford some measure of pleasure." It was Westbourne, cool, self-assured and mocking. He scanned Venetia's face penetratingly, then with a look of quick surprise and then rueful amusement swept past to Whitney. "Hello, old friend. I see you took up my invitation to visit . . . er . . . me at Ingram Place."

Francine discovered George Whitney in the doorway and began choking on the biscuit she had been nibbling at. Charles immediately began attending to her, as he had been in close conversation with her on the sofa, Whitney observed with growing rage and jealousy, and he found his head going up stiffly.

Venetia was blushing to be discovered in her breeches. She had thought that everyone would have been dispersed by now to their various amusements. "Oh," she said lamely, "I did not expect . . . I er . . . will go up and change." She turned to George. "Mr. Whitney, I believe you are acquainted with everyone present. I won't be but a . . ."

George found her hand and held it to his chest. A most fetching sight, of course, to his beloved, who looked up at this moment and discovered with a sense of horror that Mr. Whitney knew well how to be attentive to another female.

"Nonsense," said George softly. "You look just fine as you are, Venetia. And"—his voice lowered still more, so that only Westbourne standing near them could hear—"I need you." He had seen when he entered that Charles, Lord Iverness, hovered all too near Francine and that she was not welcoming him to Ingram. No doubt she felt guilty to be so caught! He turned to Westbourne. "Am I not right, Taylor? Tell her she must not leave us!" It was a gallant move to shade his disappointment in Francine's behavior.

Westbourne made Venetia a slight bow, but his eyes, oh, his eyes belied the words, and she bristled beneath his gaze. "Quite right, George. *Miss Tay*"—he emphasized the name in an effort to disclose to her that he had heard Whitney call her

Venetia—"does justice to a pair of breeches, and there is no cause on our account to hurry out of them."

Her chin was up, as was her ire. How dare he? Why the deuce should he object if George Whitney called her by her given name? She was fully capable of deciding who deserved the liberty and who did not! And his eyes! Why, they laughed at her! Yes, they did!

"So gallant," she said, not attempting to disguise the edge to her voice. "I had not thought it possible, *from you*." She swept past him and went toward Charles, who was moving toward her with a cup of tea.

"Hello, pet," said Charles, handing her the cup. "It is still hot, and I'm sure you need it after your ride." Then in a lower, more intimate voice, "I put one teaspoon of sugar . . . I remembered how you like it."

"How kind of you, Charles." She turned to George. "Mr. Whitney, will you join me in a cup of tea?"

It served to get him closer to Francine. "Thank you, no," he said, moving toward the sofa, eyeing Francine hungrily. "I have little appetite these days."

"How have you been, George?" This from Iverness. "Still dueling it out with every fool stupid enough to vex you?" There was a sardonic tone, for Charles was not pleased with Whitney's arrival on the scene. He wanted no competition for Venetia's hand, and from what he could see the two were already too friendly.

"The way George shoots, it is a very good thing

that he is not!" Westbourne laughed. "Half of London might now be under ground!"

Whitney smiled at this. "You both exaggerate. I never fight unless goaded."

"Ah, but you can be goaded!" teased Westbourne.

Francine had been sitting in something of a pout wondering how it was that George and Venetia seemed on such amicable terms with one another. She was moved at this point to get up and go to Venetia, who was at the sideboard selecting a biscuit.

"Van . . . how do you and Mr. Whitney come to know one another?"

"Why, we just met," said Venetia in some surprise.

"Really?" Francine's voice rose with a touch of disbelief.

Whitney had come up behind on the pretext of pouring himself a glass of wine, and he added, "Thank heaven Miss Tay found me!"

"Oh?" said Francine in big letters.

"I had been going around the countryside searching for Ingram Place for hours when Miss Tay came along and saved my life."

"Nonsense," put in Venetia quickly to save him the embarrassment of explaining the whole. "You would have found Ingram Place soon enough. You were not so very far off."

He thanked her with his eyes for not disclosing the circumstances of their meeting, and the expression was seen by the assembled company, and each of the onlookers reacted differently. Francine felt a surge of jealousy such as she never had known herself capable of experiencing. Charles told himself that Venetia was too in need, like himself, of a fortune to throw away the squire's inheritance for someone like George Whitney. And Westbourne . . . Westbourne went thoughtful.

Taylor Westbourne was considered by his intimates to be a knowing fellow. He had a preceptive eye that took in what the average man missed. A good look at his friend brought to his notice grass stains across the back of one shoulder. An odd thing indeed even for George Whitney's casual address. Further silent inquiry directed at Venetia as she moved about the room told him that while she did indeed look charming in her unorthodox mode of dressing, there were spots of grass stains over her knees. Just what was this? Had the two found each other in a field? Just what had they been at? Curious. Most curious. He managed to touch Whitney's elbow and say in a quiet voice, "I am not a halfling, George, so don't try to bamboozle me. What were you and Miss Tay doing? Rolling in the grass?"

George twisted around sharply and said in an angry voice, "Don't be addle-brained!"

"Oh, I assure you, I am many things, but never that," said Westbourne on a hard note.

The door opened at this point and Groomsby saved George the necessity of a reply by announcing the Honorable Ferdinand Skillington. The next few moments were spent with Venetia introducing Ferdy around to the squire's houseguests. He was not in the best of humors, for he was sadly disappointed to find Venetia was not alone.

George found the opportunity to speak with Francine near the long window overlooking the gardens, "You do not seem pleased to see me here." He waited for a response. She did not look at him, and he became desperate. "Francine!" It was an urgent whisper.

She found his hazel eyes burning when she looked up. "Why did you come?" she asked.

He stiffened. "Then you wish that I had not?"

"I did not say that!" she snapped. Out of temper and unsure why.

"What *are* you saying, Francine?" he begged.

She relented. "George, I . . . it is not that I do not want you here, but . . ."

"How can we talk in a room full of people? Come walk with me outside."

"No," she answered quietly, her light-blue eyes contemplating her fingers. "That would be most improper."

"Francine . . . you are driving me mad!"

"Oh? Am I? No doubt you think so after your blissful meeting with Venetia, for I am certain you have never said any such thing to me before!" Her jealousy was forming her words.

He did not realize it. He only knew that she seemed ready to pick a fight. He had come all this way to see her, only her, and she was not pleased. "My friendship with Miss Tay is just that, but I am not so certain about your feelings regarding Taylor!" he was moved to utter angrily.

"Oh! That is the outside of enough! He is my cousin."

"Yes, and you took pains to conceal the fact that he would be here with you at Ingram Place! Tell me, if he came up to scratch, would you have him?" He was begging her to deny it, but his tone was far too harsh for Francine to contemplate more than its sound.

"Better him than you!" she said before she realized what she was about.

He clicked his heels together formally. "Goodbye, Miss Fenton!" With which he turned and moved toward Venetia.

"Miss Tay"—he was taking up her hand—"I thank you for all your kindnesses and regret that it is time I was off."

"But . . ." she started and saw the fury written in his eyes. "Yes, of course, you must be tired." She watched him take his leave of everyone, and when the drawing-room door had closed behind him she quickly excused herself and hastily caught up to him at the front door.

"George . . ."

He turned. The door was being held open for him by Groomsby, who looked on with concealed interest. "Miss Tay? What is it?"

"Outside, sir!" she commanded and took his arm. They moved outdoors and starting walking toward the stables. "Now, tell me, what has happened? You two looked to be in the devil of bad straits!"

"It is, I believe, worse than that."

"Why?"

"Miss Fenton told me that she prefers her cousin's suit to mine," he said on a miserable note.

"Oh, I don't believe it," scoffed Venetia.

"Don't you? Well, I am not such a fool," riposted Mr. Whitney with more speed than thought. He caught himself up, blushed and begged her, taking both her now ungloved hands into his, "Miss Tay, do forgive me. I am not myself."

"Nonsense! And just a little while ago, I was Venetia."

"I took a liberty."

"You did indeed, but I didn't mind. Now"—she pulled out of his hold—"you and Francine had words. Don't you realize when a woman is upset she will say all manner of things she doesn't really mean?"

"Yes, but . . ."

"I have got to get back into the house now, for it will look odd my standing out here with you, but George . . . come by tomorrow morning. I mean to get up an expedition to Northumberland Park, and let's see if that doesn't help straighten things out between you two."

He smiled at her and flicked her pert nose. "You are turning out to be the best of good friends. Right then!" He turned and made off for the stables.

Venetia watched him for just a moment, and when she turned around toward the house, was caught by the look of Francine's face in the hall window. "Oh no," Venetia breathed out loud. Just what was Francine thinking?

She rushed into the house in time to catch her friend going up the main staircase. "Francie, wait . . ."

"I don't wish to speak with you just now, Venetia," said Francine on a cold note.

"Oh now, Francie . . ." tried Venetia.

"Please, do leave me alone." It was a tragic sound, and she gave her back to Venetia.

Miss Tay would have at that point pursued her up the stairs, but a voice at her back brought her head around.

"Venetia! So here you are," said Ferdy coming up behind her.

The front door opened and yet another male voice exploded in pleased accents, "Ferdy! By Jove, man, am I glad I've caught you before you left Ingram Place! I've just come from Skillington Hall."

"Have you?" returned Ferdy interestedly. "Why? I wasn't there, you know . . . been here."

"Well, I know that, you gapeseed!" returned Gilly. "Look, there is going to be a cockfight in Berwick-upon-Tweed, and if we rush we can make it in time to place our bets!"

"Never say so!" exclaimed Ferdy. "But it wasn't to be until next week."

"Yes, well, Havermore says his red is fit right now and means to take Jackwell's gray!" explained Gilly.

"Hold!" said Venetia, coming between her brother and Ferdy. "Now just a minute."

"Venetia, it's going to be a bang-up fight! You don't want me to miss it, and I swear I'll be back in time for dinner," said Gilly hastily.

"Of course you will, but you will also give me a moment to go up and change, for I have been wanting to go into Berwick these past two weeks, and you know you have promised me, Gilly."

"Yes, so I have, but . . . we don't have the time to wait for you to change."

"I promise you, I won't make you late for your miserable cockfight. I just mean to change into a riding habit . . . and Gilly, I can ride as fast as either of you two!"

"I am sorry to interrupt," said a strong male voice at their backs.

Venetia silently chastised herself for the effect his voice produced on her nerves. She twisted around and saw Westbourne, with Charles at his back, coming up to them. Westbourne continued after a quick, penetratingly hard look at her face, "I couldn't help but overhear that you plan to attend a cockfight?"

"Yes. It's some distance and if we are to be there, we should get started," said Gilly, flushing. He had met Westbourne briefly at breakfast and he had found him as much a Corinthian as he had been three years ago. What was more, he liked him and couldn't understand why his sister did not. Well, but then the squire had made all things so uncomfortable after that meeting. He was most flattered to have a nonesuch actually wish to join his party and added hastily, "But I would be honored to have you join us, my lord."

"Cockfights are nasty little events," put in Charles languidly, "but they do serve to while away the hours. I shall get my hat and gloves."

"Ferdy," called Venetia as she mounted the stairs, "don't you let them leave without me. I want to visit Nanny, and Gilly promised!"

"You may depend upon me, Venetia!" called Ferdy gallantly.

Westbourne eyed the young man. In earnest, yes, but only infatuated. Would the cunning Miss Tay use the poor lad? She seemed capable of almost anything. Hadn't she already managed to somehow interest George? And just how did they happen to meet? There was more to that than could be scratched up on the surface! The girl seemed to be playing poker, and she was good at it. She didn't discard and she didn't let you read her eyes, and when she did, they were all innocence! But he, Lord Westbourne, knew better!

Chapter Nine

"In four strides from the first to the second!" said Gilly confidently. "You can't do it on that old nag of yours!"

"Nag?" returned Ferdy, bristling. "Hank is a trooper and can do it in four if yours can!"

"Right then," started Gilly, preparing for the double jump.

"Hold!" cried Charles, taking charge of this. "You'll have to trot in and then canter the next . . . and if I were you I'd put a wager on it, Gilly, for I've watched Ferdy's mount and the poor old thing hasn't got the timing."

Venetia laughed, and her green eyes sparkled. "Leave it to Gilly to turn a mishap into a frolic! First he insists we take this shortcut through the woods and now he is playing games. If he keeps this up, you will all miss the cockfight."

Westbourne found himself mesmerized by her. Perhaps it was the striking contrast of her long white-gold hair beneath her apple-green silk top hat. Perhaps it was the lines of the apple-green riding habit against her well-shaped body, or the brilliance of her green eyes. Perhaps it was the way she rode her mare.

He shook himself and said lightly, "You said something earlier about visiting a . . . nanny in Berwick?" It was a question more for the sport of conversation, and it was with some surprise that he discovered he had a certain interest in her reply.

"Yes. Gilly should visit with her too," said Venetia, growing suddenly wistful. "Sweet Doobie . . ." Then, bringing herself back to the present, "Mrs. Doobie was my mother's nanny, you see, and when my parents died, she had already been pensioned, for both Gilly and I were already grown." Again she had to shake off the past. "Well, for some ridiculous reason the squire has never allowed me to go the distance alone to Berwick, and Gilly is forever busy these days with one thing or another."

"I see," said Westbourne. His eyes scanned her face, and he felt touched to the heart. He shrugged the sensation off and laughed. "My uncle, however, allows you to romp about in breeches quite unattended? How contrary of him."

She glittered sheepishly, and he was struck by the impish quality of her charm. "I don't tell him, you see, but then I am never gone overlong, so he has no cause for concern." Gilly was taking the jump, and she pointed. "He shouldn't tease Ferdy so, for Ferdy has never had enough control over his gelding, and that jump Gilly has set up is rather high. Oh look, one, two, three, four . . ."

"Good lad!" exclaimed Westbourne. "Well done."

"Aye," agreed Charles. "Now for you, my buck," he said at Ferdy.

The Honorable Ferdinand Skillington took in breath, set his gelding into a trot and rushed the first log jump, but Ferdy then forgot to stay up, forgot to give his release, and when the bay began to refuse, it was a bit late to crop him, but crop him he did, which did get them over the jump, but they had done it in five strides.

"Pay up!" cried Gilly gleefully.

"Eh, and so I shall," said Ferdy, pulling a bill out of his inner pocket. "But I'd swear that second jump has had a branch or two added to it since the last time we took this trail."

"So it has," assented Gilly amicably. "Raised it about nine inches meself just the other day . . . see there . . ." But Ferdy was already charging after him, crop raised in the air and meant for his friend's head.

The remaining company laughed at the scene and followed, taking the jumps easily and lightly and acknowledging each other's skill in silent admiration. When they slowed to a trot and found the main pike, it was with Charles riding beside Venetia and Westbourne bringing up the rear.

"That Gilly of yours is something of a gull-catcher," said Charles amiably with no insult intended, for he meant to have Venetia and his uncle's inheritance, and every minute spent in her company confirmed this desire.

"Yes, he has ever been a prankster." She sighed. "But there is no harm in him, you know."

"I wouldn't believe it even if you swore that there was," returned Charles, and his smile caressed her face.

"What that halfling of yours wants is something steady to occupy his time," said Westbourne thoughtfully.

She turned and contemplated him for a long moment. "Odd that you should say so. It is what I have thought more often than not."

Charles's eyes narrowed, "Yes, Taylor, how perceptive of you."

"Have you ever thought of sending him off to London? Perhaps he could find work in the home office. Or doesn't he have a mind to politics?" pursued Westbourne, again taking the lady's attention.

"Oh, my lord, that would be perfect for him, but he does not come of age for another three years . . . and it would be difficult for him. You see, he is reluctant to leave me until I am . . ." she turned away in some confusion.

"Naturally the lad doesn't want to leave his sister until she has been comfortably settled," said Charles on a long drawl, indicating to a nicety, he felt, the obtuseness of Westbourne's line of conversation.

"Which, of course, brings me back to that nagging question," said Westbourne softly. He ignored Charles, and his eyes flirted outrageously with his quarry. "Just how do you happen to move about unspoken for?"

She laughed, and it was a bright musical sound.

"It is a very simple matter. I haven't accepted the offers—not that they have been numerous—that were presented to me. Now, don't be thinking I haven't been launched, for when my Aunt Gussie was alive, we were wont to enjoy ourselves at the country dances."

"No one caught your fancy?" pursued Westbourne.

"A doltish question!" snapped Charles. "If someone had, we wouldn't now have the pleasure of her company!"

"That is not necessarily the case," returned Westbourne quietly.

"No, it is not for some, but it is a good enough answer for the present," said Venetia, putting an end to the inquisition about her status.

Westbourne still felt inclined to pursue this avenue, for without delving into the whys, he wanted to know exactly how Venetia came to be unattached at three and twenty. However, he could see that with Charles closing in, it would be an impossible task at the moment, so he allowed it to drop. As it happened, Lord Iverness set himself to be a charming fellow for the remainder of the journey, and silently Westbourne acknowledged his cousin to be a pleasant companion, at least when it suited him.

Charles had summed up the situation for himself. He could see that Taylor was playing some sort of game with Venetia. What it was he could not decide, but of one thing he was certain—he was not about to let Westbourne have her! Let Taylor take Francine! He was a cunning fellow, and his instincts told him that the squire cared for

Venetia Tay and to her would go the major share of his estate.

So it was in a jesting mood that they all entered the old world town of Berwick.

"Gilly, do let us pass the old bridge," cried Venetia excitedly. She turned, her green eyes beaming to Westbourne riding beside her. "Have you ever been to Berwick bridge? It is the quaintest thing imaginable, quite, quite lovely."

"Oh, its just an old bridge," complained Gilly.

"Absurd boy!" Venetia laughed. "It dates back to the seventeenth century."

"I had not realized you were interested in the history of our weathered old land," said Westbourne softly. He found that he wanted to get into her mind. There was so much about her that was an enigma to him, so much that did not jibe with his initial impression of her character.

She blushed in some confusion. "Well, I am no bluestocking, my lord, but there is something about the past that has always caught my interest."

"Yes, I have always found it to be so . . . the ruins of a castle, the remains of an abbey. Albion is full of mysteries," agreed Westbourne softly.

He was cut off by Charles, who felt suddenly excluded from the conversation. "Ha! The only mysteries Taylor is drawn to are dealt over the table at a gaming hell!"

Westbourne ignored him. "Berwick," he said on a low note, his gray eyes meeting Venetia's inquiring look, "is a border town, I believe, very rich in Elizabethan walls?"

"That's right," said Venetia, quite amazed that Westbourne should know such a thing; it occurred to her that she might be wrong in her summation of his character. "Look, here is the first of the three seventeenth-century bridges. Isn't it magnificent?"

"Aye," agreed Ferdy. "For if you look below you'll spot the finest, fattest salmon in all the county!"

He had succeeded very well in drawing Venetia's attention, for she and the assembled company fell into tolerant amusement, and it was in this festive mood that they arrived some moments later at a small but well-kept cottage of gray stone.

Iverness managed to bolt off his horse first and reach Venetia's side just as she was about to dismount. However, Ferdy was quick to flank her, and thus she was seen off.

"Go ahead," said Taylor. "I think your nanny might want to see you too. I'll mind the horses," said Westbourne to Gilly as he bent to take up the reins of the abandoned animals.

Gilly sighed. "I suppose she'll put up a fuss if I don't go in for a moment. But I'll send Ferdy back to help you with the horses."

Westbourne watched as the undersized red-painted door of the cottage opened and a diminutive woman, frail, mop-capped and elderly, appeared. He watched as she gleefully took Venetia into her arms, opened them again and pulled Gilly along with her.

All this was quite unexpected. He watched as Ferdy and Charles bowed themselves off and started back toward him. Venetia had looked like a lost little girl as she dove into her nanny's arms. Odd. She had always seemed, from the first moment of their meeting, such a capable, strong and wielding maid. It just didn't fit with the scheming, grabbing, cunning creature he had assumed (from what he believed were her actions) her to be. Perhaps he had been wrong? No. His uncle's proposed will indicated that she was definitely all these things. Perhaps his initial impression needed modification, though. Perhaps some revision of his opinion was called for; after all, maybe there were extenuating circumstances that had forced her into mercernary actions. However, he still cautioned himself, for in the end, whatever her reasons, she was still moved by her need for financial advancement!

Cits, merchants, seamen, young and elderly gentlemen all, were gathered in the open-air court for the grand occasion known as the cockfight. Voices were raised in bold octaves and everyone seemed to be talking at once.

Betting was rife and ale was being liberally imbibed. It was a man's world, and nearly each and every man was embarked wholeheartedly on displaying how completely he belonged there. Lord Iverness gave this consideration little attention, however. He was there because it was an opportunity to win some cash, and it was with some pride that he congratulated himself on the wisdom of his wagers. He had certainly been wise when he had put his money on the gray cock, for that bet was about to pay handsomely. Damn, but it would feel good to have some loose ready in his pockets for a change! Where the others of his company had gone off to did not at that moment concern him. He meant to keep an eye on the various individuals he had placed wagers with, for in addition to the hefty sum he had put down in the betting book, he had invested freely within the ranks of the hubbub and taken on anyone who would give him attractive odds. The gray was not a favorite, and odds indeed he did receive!

Ferdy and Gilly were at that moment in the very midst of battle. This in spite of the fact that Gilly was about to win a sizable amount for his bet on the gray. Ferdy, on the other hand, was about to lose a very great sum. Ferdy was not as a rule a sore loser, and may be excused his lapse in this affair for an excellent reason. When they had started out, they had been much in accord on one thing: Both Gilly and Ferdy staunchly believed that the red contender had the affair neatly in hand. It was as plain as pikestaff that this was so, and therefore Gilly surprised himself when at the last minute he placed his bet in the book on the gray. Being a faithful friend he did not do such a dastardly thing to Ferdy, but put in Ferdy's bet as they had earlier agreed. So there was Ferdy demanding retribution in one form or another.

Westbourne looked on the two youngsters' antics with a great deal of tolerant amusement, however, for the past twenty minutes he had spent nearly as much time looking up at the sky, and what he observed brought a frown to his eyes. If he was not much mistaken about northern weather, they were due for a heavy shower. Now, for himself, he did not mind, nor would the assembled company. They would collect their winnings within the hour and be off to fetch Venetia.

It would not be the first time he had been caught in the rain. Venetia? Her habit was made of a lovely silk. He wondered ruefully what she had had to do to connive its expenditure out of his uncle. But never mind, there was a simple solution.

"Gilly," he interrupted Ferdy with his hand held up for a moment, "look . . . you and Ferdy collect what is due to me from the betting book, find Iverness and follow me to Ingram Place as soon as possible. I think we are in for a bolt of rain."

"Yes, but . . ." started Gilly.

"I mean to hire a curricle and take up your sister."

"Splendid notion. You can have them keep dinner warm for us up at the house, for if it means to rain, we shall be delayed."

"Right," said Westbourne, who was already off.

"What's this?" stuck in Ferdy, diverted for the moment from his purpose as he watched Westbourne take his leave. "Devil a bit, Gilly! What the deuce have you done?"

"Take a damper, Ferdy," said Gilly amicably.

"I will not! Are you daft? Just tell me, did I just hear you give that . . . that London beau leave to drive Venetia home alone?"

"You did," answered Gilly. "Now lower your voice, infant!" He shook his head. "Do you want Venetia getting drenched in the rain?"

"No, and I don't want her getting seduced in a carriage!"

Gilly stared down his friend for a long moment while he composed himself. "Oh, and I suppose you think *I* do?" His tone was ominous.

Ferdy clearly saw his mistake and stammered, "Now, that's not what I mean, so you needn't bristle up at me, Gilly! Look, you know as well as I do that Westbourne is a Corinthian, a nonesuch, a . . . well, he has been on the town forever. Near to thirty he is. And Venetia, you know, Venetia . . . could have her head turned."

"That's how much you know of Venetia! Make yourself easy, Ferdy, she won't have him. She don't even like him. But down, lad, she won't have you either!"

"Know that, Gilly?"

"As a matter of fact, yes, I do, so button up and let's attend to the problem at hand. The gray has won us a pretty penny, enough to cover your loss and keep us plump in the pocket for quite some time to come."

"And that's another thing . . ." started Ferdy, but he had his arm suddenly taken up as Gilly released a laugh and pulled him along with him.

Chapter Ten

Francine Fenton pulled her pretty pink cashmere shawl around her shoulders and glanced up at the sky. It looked as though it might rain soon. A sigh. She should have gone with them to Berwick. Venetia had rushed into her room as though absolutely nothing had gone wrong between them. How lovely she had looked in her apple green habit. It was no wonder that George had been smitten with her. Venetia? Venetia had seemed unaware . . . and indeed perhaps it hadn't been her fault, but she had received her coldly.

"Come on, Francine . . . the ride to Berwick will do you good, and I shall be happy for your company. You will like Doobie. She is a treasure of wisdom."

"Oh? And I suppose you think I need to rely on

your Doobie's advice?" It was stiffly said and meant as an end to the discussion.

Venetia frowned. She had never seen Francine so out of temper and intractable before. She touched Francine's hand. "Francie? I don't know what poor George has said to put you in such a miff, but . . ."

"Ooh!" snapped Francine. "Poor George, is it? You two seem to have forgotten the proprieties in your whirlwind affair! I am sure I did not call Mr. Whitney by his first name for at least a month after our initial meeting!"

Venetia blushed. "Yes, I suppose up here in the wilds, the formalities sometimes are thrown to the winds . . . but what you can mean by 'our whirlwind affair,' I am certain I don't know. In fact, Francine, I am a little surprised by your attitude."

"Are you?" Inwardly Francine felt she was in the wrong, and she softened. "Well, perhaps I am just out of sorts. Why don't you go and visit with your nanny, and leave me to myself for a bit. I wouldn't be very good company anyway."

"Are you sure, Francie?"

"Quite."

So it was that Miss Fenton had watched Venetia depart, and the moment the party had left, she knew she had behaved idiotically. She attempted to amuse herself with various occupations of a sedentary nature and finally took up her shawl and meandered out of doors.

The sound of carriage wheels at her back brought her head around, and she discovered coming toward her a neatly if somewhat somberly attired gentleman in an open curricle led by one piebald. He reined in and tipped his top hat to her. "Hello," he said hesitatingly. "I hope you won't mind if I introduce myself? I am the vicar, John Qerkdon."

"Oh yes, I have heard Venetia speak of you. How do you do?"

His face brightened. "Venetia mentioned me? How nice. Forgive me, am I to assume that you are Miss Fenton?"

"Yes sir, I am."

He was jumping down, going to his horse's head. "I am on my way up to the house, Miss Fenton. Would you allow me to drive you?"

"Thank you. It has grown quite chilly."

He helped her into the carriage, saw her seated, and quickly went around to mount and take up the reins. "Venetia is, I suppose, at home?"

"Oh, I am sorry, have you come to visit with Venetia?"

He smiled indulgently, for he assumed that she must by now realize he was Venetia's most ardent suitor. "Why, yes . . . with Venetia and the squire, if he is taking visitors . . ."

"Oh dear, I am afraid that the squire is not seeing anyone and Venetia is not home."

"Ooh?" Elongated and thoughtful. "Not home, you say? No doubt she is visiting with one of the squire's tenants?"

"No, she has gone into Berwick to visit with her retired nanny."

"Alone?" the vicar squeaked out, for he had been afraid of this. Venetia had mentioned more than once that she wanted to visit with Doobie and that she was tired of waiting for Gilly to accompany her.

"Oh no, Gilly and my cousins, as well as Mr. Skillington, were with her."

"Indeed!" said the vicar, and he was no more pleased than he had been when he had feared she had made the trip alone. They had pulled up in front of the Ingram's heavily molded front door.

On the other side of that door an interesting conversation between George Whitney and Groomsby was taking place, for George had been unable to sit comfortably at the inn, knowing that his darling Francine was displeased with him.

"Not in, you say, Groomsby? How odd. I did not pass her on the drive when I rode up here," said Mr. Whitney doubtfully.

"She went outdoors some ten minutes ago, sir. The grounds *are* quite extensive."

"Yes, well then, I'll just go out and see if I can catch sight of her."

"Very good, sir," said Groomsby, opening the door.

Eyes can lie so well. What one sees with one's own eyes is not always what it appears. However, in the fleeting passing of a moment, one does not consider this, and such was the case as Mr. Whitney's jaw dropped and his hazel eyes widened in outraged surprise.

This because, as the door of Ingram Place was opening, the good vicar's arms were outstretched to receive Miss Fenton and help her alight from his curricle. The hem of her gown got caught on the rough edging of its first step. He clucked and reached around to free her. "Hold there, Miss

Fenton, a moment or your lovely gown will be torn."

She was forced to rest one delicate hand on his shoulder as his ministrations threw her somewhat off balance. Far too aware of the fact that the proximaty of their bodies offended all the purer proprieties, she was a bit hasty when she finally made her descent. The net result of this was to send her tumbling with a screech of fear into the vicar's arms.

George and Groomsby were by this time in the open doorway, one watching with growing wrath and the other with a great deal of misgiving. Had Mr. Whitney a sword it would have been drawn. Instead, he had with him his fists, which he placed into position as he stampeded down the steps.

"Unhand her, you swine!" commanded George as he neatly landed a pretty left hook full into the vicar's face.

George's facer had drawn the vicar's cork, and Qerkdon's hand flew to his bloodied nose. "Blister it man, you've broken my nose!" he cried.

Francine saw the blood running, took the vicar at his word and did what any gently bred maid of her quiet sensibilities would do; she fainted.

George swore beneath his breath that he would do the villain in for this day's work, and with these ominous words went to his knees beside Miss Fenton's limp body.

Groomsby came to the rescue by quickly ushering the vicar into the house with the promise of care and the assurance that he was fairly certain that the vicar's nose was quite unbroken.

"That may be so, but my shirt has been ruined

by that madman!" expostulated Qerkdon, hastily looking back at his attacker.

"Easy now, sir, for we don't want him following up on that left of his, now do we?"

"No, no . . . but why should he do such a thing? Who is he, and is he, do you think"—he lowered his voice—"queer in the attic?"

"He is Mr. Whitney, vicar . . . and I dunno . . . not daft, no, but near to it." Groomsby sighed. "Word has it he is dotty on Miss Fenton." He showed the vicar to the library. "There now, make yourself easy near the fire and I'll be bringing ye a basin of warm water and we'll attend to that nose of yers."

Whitney had by this time taken up his Francine into his arms and noted to himself that this was a deed he had performed with far more ease in his fantasies. Nevertheless, he did justice to the romantic reputation he had acquired over the years by neatly cradling her as he carried her to the library in Groomsby's wake.

The first drops of rain had begun to fall as Westbourne led Miss Tay to the waiting carriage. She stopped a moment as he opened the door wide for her and looked full into his handsome face. It was a mistake, for she could feel herself shaken by the sudden intensity of his gray eyes.

"What is it, Miss Tay?" he asked, for she had not spoken.

From the corner of her eye she could see Doobie at the window watching. Doobie had taken to his lordship at once, and Venetia had admitted to herself that he could be very charming when he chose, and for some obscure reason he had chosen to win over her perceptive nanny. "This . . . this was unnecessary," she somehow stammered out. She hadn't been able to say very much from the moment he had appeared at the cottage with the driver and the closed carriage. After all, she had just finished a ripping diatribe on Lord Westbourne's arrogance to Doobie and then there he was being solicitous! It was the outside of enough, really!

"Nonsense," said Westbourne softly, for instinctively he knew he had taken over the reins with this last maneuver, though truth was that had not been his purpose. "It was very necessary if we were going to keep you dry." He took her arm and aided her as she took the step up and found herself in a small and rather cozy closed carriage.

A moment later he was seated beside her and giving the signal to the driver to move on. "There," he said, taking up the fur rug and placing it over her lap. "That's better."

This was too much, and Miss Tay found her tongue. "Oh, stop it! You are really coming on sweet, aren't you? Well, I am not as green as all that, I do assure you!"

"Now, what can you mean?" He feigned innocence.

"Oh, capital!" returned the lady, incensed. "Now he is the round-eyed boy, as though he had never accused me of scheming for his uncle's money!" she said as though speaking to another person. Her green eyes blazed, and even in the growing dusk, he could see them well.

"What has my opinion of your behavior got to do with the fact that as a gentleman I would not allow a lady in my company, who is also a relation—or rather, a connection—be caught in a rainstorm?"

"Why didn't Gilly come for me?" she threw at him, piqued, for he had not denied that he thought ill of her.

"I suggested to him that he remain behind to collect our winnings and my cousin, Charles."

"You lost Charles?"

"Never fear, precious, he was not lost, only out of sight. He will, of course, be in a wild rage when he discovers that I have had the forethought and now the pleasure of collecting you for the return journey." With this he allowed himself a hearty chuckle.

"Oh, so that is it! You have played the gentleman only to better your cousin! Why you *are* despicable."

"No, no, you wrong me, love. I came for you . . . because I wanted to. The thought that my having done so will enrage Charles is only an added bonus!"

"Oh, you are horrid! To laugh over the fact that you have upset someone." She was shaking her head.

"I have it on excellent authority that laughing is the sign of a rational animal."

She cut him off and pushed into her corner away from him. "More animal than rational when you laugh at someone's distress!"

He leaned closer to her and was amused by the fact that even in the dim light he could see her blushing. "You cut me to the quick. But here, let us leave off our jousting and be serious for a moment."

"Oh, is that possible?" She was cocking her head, and her arched brow matched the sarcasm in her voice.

"Perhaps, if you will be honest?"

"Oooh, why . . . I could hit you! If I were a man, I would call you out! It is easy for you to take advantage, isn't it? You don't think twice when you know your victim is . . ."

"Have I been the bully?" He was frowning.

"You know that you have," she snapped and looked away from him to find her own profile reflected in her window. Past her reflection she could see his. How thoughtful he looked with his hand to his chin in consideration of her words.

"Right then, I shall start over. We shall give one another the benefit of the doubt and assume that we are both being honest."

"If I cannot be honest with you, my lord, I will not answer you," she said softly.

He touched her nose and found his finger straying to her cheek. She didn't move, but he saw her eyes grow wary, and he laughed lightly. "Such kitten eyes, cautious, mischievous. If a man weren't learned in such things, he could fall." His voice was soft, low, and held a quality that sent a thrill through Venetia's limbs.

She felt very nearly spellbound by his warm gray eyes, his all too seductive voice, and knew a moment's desire to give herself over to his earnest flirtation. She did not in fact retreat from him, and said in a low voice, her eyes full on his face, "However, *you* are a learned man and know better." It was a statement, but something inside of her wanted him to refute it.

Somehow his arm had found its way around her delicate shoulders, somehow she found him now very close, and his lips moved so very near her own. His words were a whisper, husky, tantalizing.

"Oh, I know better, but at this moment, I could easily forget." All he wanted was that luscious mouth of hers. He was hungry for it, knew an urgency he could not put aside, and he bent almost wildly to have her. He was an experienced man, and when he felt her stiffen he immediately gentled his onslaught. Oh Lord, but the feel of her in his arms was nearly more than he could bear. He wanted more. . . .

What was happening? Was she letting Westbourne kiss her? How could she so forget herself? Oh, but the sky was bright with rockets and her body felt so delicious in his arms, and stop! She put up her hand and pushed hard. "Taylor!" she objected in what she hoped was an authoritative voice.

He brought himself up. What he needed was air. Devil take it, what was going on? He could not remember ever finding himself so lost in a woman before. What was it about her? He stared at her a long thoughtful moment, attempting perhaps to resolve this problem, but all that happened was that he found himself delving even deeper into her green eyes.

He looked away and said quietly, "I'm sorry." It was almost a curt sound.

"Are you?" she returned, and because she wanted to break the spell of the moment, find her ground again and stand without wobbling, she allowed the tease to enter the words. She felt guilty in the act. After all, she had allowed him to kiss her, hadn't she?

He turned sharply to look at her, and then a slow grin spread over his face. Damn, but she was unlike any other. "Oh yes," he said softly. "More than you can realize."

"You seem to have a talent for insulting me. First you kiss me, sir, and then you tell me you are sorry for it!" She laughed lightly. "Well then, we have established that you are man, handsome and virile, and I am woman, soft and almost pliable. Now, perhaps we may move on to the matter at hand."

"What a very interesting way of putting it. But tell me precious, must we move on . . ." Again he was coming closer, touching her chin.

"Hhmmm . . ." She sighed. "You see, I don't like you, my lord, and even if I did, it wouldn't change the fact that you are about to announce your engagement to Francine . . . that is, if she will have you over George!"

He snorted and sat back to stare at her. "You make astounding assumptions, Miss Tay."

"Do I? What is so astounding about it? It is a well-known fact that you must inherit your uncle's money in order to come about, and as I won't have you . . ."

"My love, I haven't asked you," he put it gently, his eyes twinkling.

"Well, even if you did, and besides, that is sidestepping the point. Now, allow me to proceed."

He hung his head meekly. "Indeed, I do beg your pardon."

"It appears that you must pursue poor Francie, who does not, at least I do not think she does, love you." Venetia shook her head. "And I cannot blame her." This time the twinkle was in her eyes and they glimmered in the dusky setting of their closed quarters.

He was unable to restrain the twinge of amusement that marked his tone, though he dearly wanted to box her ears for the insult.

"Disposing of me in this manner, you have then settled it in your head to have my cousin, Charles?"

"He is very . . . gallant, and I have enjoyed his company these two days, but as to marriage? That is quite another thing, isn't it?"

"Is it?" His voice was dry.

"Odd as it may sound to you sir, I would like to be in love with the man I am to marry. You know, the storybook kind."

"You have a talent for almost making me believe you," he said quietly.

"Oh, go to the devil!" she retorted in some heat.

Again he moved to take her in his arms and was surprised to find she made no effort to resist. His voice when it came against her ears was low and seductive. "If you will promise to go with me, love . . . I might consider the trip."

"Stop it!" She shook her head and leaned her body away from him, gently pulling now to be free, "No doubt your conceit comes of being an only son!"

He put up a brow. "I was no such thing!" Then

he was releasing her, looking away. "I had a brother, you know . . . an older brother."

She saw the darkling look set his gray eyes and became curious. "What . . . what happened?" her question was bold, and she wouldn't have blamed him if he had rebuffed her.

He didn't. He wanted to answer her. Odd, that. Why should he? he asked himself, but he looked at her full. "My brother was the best of good men. He died for his country at Waterloo." Again he looked away. "I lost all of them there . . . brother, father, mother."

"Oh . . . how terrible. I . . . I am so sorry, Taylor."

He turned back to her. "Enough of me. It is you I want to talk about. Tell me, Venetia . . . will you marry Charles to secure your future?"

"How can I?"

"It is what society expects of you."

She snapped her fingers in the air, "So much for society."

"Then you don't mean to have him?"

She smiled mysteriously, then, "Oh, I didn't say that. I said I wouldn't allow society to dictate who my husband will be." More than that she wasn't about to tell him.

Chapter Eleven

The squire's nightcap went askew as he shook his head in a distempered fit. "I will know what is happening in my own home! Groomsby, do you hear, I will know and I will know now!"

"Of course, sir, but . . ." started Groomsby, stalling for time to think.

"Don't bleat at me, you addle-brained twig! I've issued an ultimatum and will know how it fares! Does my nephew make up to Venetia?"

"As to that, I am sure Lord Iverness is very attentive to Miss Venetia," said Groomsby warily.

"Dolt! Do I pay you to spurt fustian at me? You know very well I mean Taylor. I have fancied Taylor for Venetia ever since my Gussie died. She would have liked the match and *I* like the match, so tell me, *is there a match?*" His feeble hand formed a fist, and he attacked his cumbersome bed linens with zeal.

Groomsby had known exactly what his squire wished to discover and had hoped to evade the issue by interesting Ingram in the fact that Iverness was courting Venetia. Gently he said, "I am sorry sir, I haven't really noticed. Had I realized that you—"

"Fool!" interrupted the squire. "Don't think you can bamboozle me! I may have one foot in m'grave, but the other is right here." He went silent for a long moment and pulled at his lower lip. "Ha!" he croaked suddenly. "No doubt they've been at each other's throats. Fine. Fine. Do you think it could be otherwise with such as they?"

"I . . . I don't think I understand, squire," returned Groomsby.

"No, of course you don't. Go on . . . get out and send Venetia to me." He fell back upon his pillow, wearied by his exertions.

Groomsby frowned. The squire had tired himself. Now what to do? Venetia was not home yet, and he wondered if this information would upset the squire further. "I am afraid, sir, I can't do that just yet."

"*Can't?* Can't?" returned the squire, sitting up again. "Why the flaming . . ."

Groomsby quickly interrupted lest the squire work himself into a tither again. "There now, squire, perhaps that's miss now, for I hear horses on the front drive."

"Oh, and where was miss?" returned Ingram sharply.

"With Lord Westbourne, I believe," returned Groomsby hurriedly, hoping to appease.

He did. It worked like a charm. "Eh? With Taylor, you say? Good, good, have them both come up to visit with me. But Groomsby . . . give me some time to rest a bit. . . ." Again he was sinking into his pillow.

"Yes, squire, of course." Devoutly Groomsby hoped that Miss Venetia had returned.

Francine came out of her faint rather slowly, one hand to her forehead as she surveyed George's face. "What? Oh . . . yes . . . I remember. George . . . you were a beast!"

He got off his one knee and stood up, his face flushing furiously.

"I? I am a beast? Am I to understand that you encouraged that man's advances?" One hand pointed at the vicar, who had his head back and a handkerchief poised at his injured nose.

"What are you talking about? You are absurd!" retorted the lady.

"Am I? I find you screaming, I find him clutching you in his arms, and *I am the one* who is absurd?"

"The vicar was not clutching me in his arms!" riposted Francine in shocked accents.

"I am very glad to hear it," said Venetia merrily, coming into the room with Taylor at her back.

Westbourne surveyed the assembled company, eyed the vicar curiously a moment and closed the door before taking up position by the sideboard, where he seemed busy enough with pouring himself a glass of brandy. "Venetia?" he said quietly, for she had not yet moved far away from him. "May I pour you a glass of Madeira?"

"No, thank you, my lord." Her attention was all for the vicar, and she went to him, for he was jumping to his feet. "John, what has happened to you? No, do sit down . . . yes, and leave your head back, or your nose will start to bleed again."

He took her hand and pulled her down on the sofa beside him. "I am so glad you are here, Venetia. Perhaps you may bring that scoundrel to his senses."

Venetia gently pushed the vicar's head back. "Scoundrel?" She laughed. "Do you mean George? Nonsense." She looked at Francine. "Francie, what has been happening here?"

Francine sat up and twisted her fingers together. "Oh, Venetia, George gave the vicar a bloody nose, and he isn't even sorry."

"Well, I can see that George has given John a bloody nose." Her hand waved at George to silence him. "But Francine, we both know that he could not have done so unless he thought he had reason."

"That's right!" snapped George. "But she will only think the worst of me!"

"And you?" cried Francine on a sob. "What did you think of me? That I would throw myself into a strange man's arms?"

"No, Miss Fenton, I thought you were being attacked," said George heatedly.

"What? At my uncle's front door?" said the lady reasonably.

"You screamed!" answered Mr. Whitney, by now nearly ready to burst and hit anything in sight.

"I tripped and fell, and the vicar caught me, you

big dunce!" said Francine and then bit her lip, for she could see the hurt descend into George's eyes. Many things she might call him, but she had gone too far to do so in the presence of two other gentlemen.

He stiffened, made a bow and started to take his leave, but Venetia got to her feet and within a few strides had his arm, "*No!* Now I have had enough of all this. You heard Francine scream, you saw her in John's arms . . ." With this she turned, her eyes brim full, her tone teasing. "I must say, John, I am surprised at you."

"Venetia . . . believe me . . ." started the vicar.

"I do." Venetia laughed. "Head back." She proceeded, still holding George's arm. "You acted quickly, before thinking, but you did it out of the purest of intentions, and I shan't have you leave here on the outs with both Francine and my very good friend Vicar John Qerkdon."

Silently, Westbourne applauded. Feebly, George repeated, "Vicar?" George blushed darkly and attempted to catch some breath.

"That's right. Now come with me." She took him to the vicar, and had the situation in command. "John, I have the pleasure of introducing to you Mr. George Whitney, and I hope you two may yet turn out to be good friends, as I believe Mr. Whitney plans to visit us here at Ingram Place quite frequently."

The vicar considered George for a long moment and said on a bit of a whining note, "You nearly broke my nose!"

Westbourne was there, handing George a glass of brandy. "But he didn't . . . so I suppose you must thank him," said Taylor lightly and did what he set out to accomplish. The company gave themselves over to uneasy mirth, but it was enough to dispel some of the acrid air.

"I acted rashly, vicar, and do beg your pardon," said George after a moment.

"Eh? Very well," conceded the vicar, looking toward Westbourne.

With a smile and a look of thanks to Westbourne, Venetia made the introductions between Taylor and the vicar. His lordship had not missed the intimacy with which Venetia handled the vicar. He had not missed the fact that the vicar held her in some esteem, and he was acutely aware of an irritation, some might have called jealousy.

Another interruption occurred to turn a questionable situation into something of a lively party, for Gilly, Ferdy and Lord Iverness arrived on the scene. Venetia invited Ferdy, George and the vicar to dine with them, and all three gentlemen seemed anxious to accept. She excused herself and went off to speak with Cook about the increased number of people she would have to set a place for, knowing it was not going to be an easy job. She was not wrong in this assumption and stood by patiently as Cook affectionately chastised her for disobeying the squire's standing rule on dinner parties.

"If ever there was a lickpenny . . . but there, it doesn't do no good complaining; that's the way things be, and you'll only find yourself on the outs by taking it on your shoulders to do the pretty!"

"I know, dearest Bess, but don't worry about me, I shall deal with the squire."

"Well, and this time you won't have to, because as it chances I've got a roast on and it's big enough to serve as a main course. Go on, then . . . I've got some work to whip up some of those Frenchie quiche tarts that young Skillington likes and as it happens will do nicely for a side dish."

Venetia laughed, planted an affectionate kiss upon Cook's plump cheek and turned to find Groomsby considering them thoughtfully.

"Well, Groomsby . . . whatever has you looking so blue?"

"Naught."

"Tell me," insisted Venetia. "You know you will in the end, so don't make me beg, Groomsby. What is it?"

"Naught. Now go on, your guests will be waiting on ye and getting into mischief."

She sighed, for it was true. There was no saying what George and the others were at by now. What a strange conglomeration the squire had in his house this evening. And how was she to manage George's wild temper? It wasn't going to be easy, not with Francine acting so unlike herself and cutting up George's peace of mind.

In spite of her misgivings she managed very neatly. This she did by putting Charles on one side of her and George on the other and dividing her attention between the two. This was necessary, for Francine took it in her head to give most of her attention to Taylor, for though Venetia had seated Francine on the other side of George, Taylor had taken up her other flank. Conversation was lively, somewhat at odds and very often near to dangerous, but Venetia found herself greatly amused.

During one of these free-flowing, unhampered, improper discussions she looked up to find Westbourne's gray eyes glinting at her. They shared a silent laugh together, and she felt a kindling warmth touch the tips of her toes and make its way through her veins, hotly, swiftly and most conqueringly, until her throat constricted and she was struck dumb. Conversation faded to the background. Charles was saying something about whisky, but his voice drowned in the thumping of her heart and she could see only Westbourne, feel only Westbourne as his gray eyes scorched her. Stop! What the deuce was this?

Too confused by this sensation to own it to herself as real, she tore her glance away from Westbourne's handsome, all too handsome, face. Listen to the discussion, get back into the discussion at hand! Ignore him, she told herself. It is naught. Naught ... you are three and twenty and ready for a man to make love to you. That is all. Your body awakens to him, and why not? He is sophisticated and virile. Repressed passion—he works his charm to release your passion, that is all, nothing else. Avoid his eyes. What is Gilly saying?

"Smugglers have been at their trade for centuries and, why? Because the taxes on the items they smuggle are outrageous and create a market," said Gilly. "And what's more, don't tell me even you, vicar, haven't bought, now and then, a flask of whisky from Scotland that never saw a custom house!"

Vicar Qerkdon flushed. "Well . . . as to that . . ."

"Stuff and nonsense!" scoffed Ferdy. "It is one thing to buy the goods and quite another to stand buff for one of the devils! And that is what you are doing, Gilly, defending them."

"Ha!" replied Gilly, firing up. "Well, my self-righteous friend, answer me this. Your land bends with the Tweed in more than one place, and don't tell me you haven't caught a glimpse of a smuggler's skiff and—"

"Yes, but that is quite another thing," put in Ferdy, quickly cutting in.

"Did you report your sighting?" demanded Gilly.

"No, but—"

"Then my point is taken. You have behaved abominably by your own set of rules, yet you would condemn starving men for making a living and robbing no one but the very rich," said Gilly smugly.

"Gilly, you cannot mean that you approve?" asked Venetia doubtfully.

"I don't understand any of this," said Francine on a puzzled note. "What can smugglers be doing in Northumberland?"

"Oh, I fancy the flaskers do well in Northumberland," said George thoughtfully. "Eh, Taylor?"

"Whisky, Francine," answered Taylor, and for a brief moment his gray eyes scanned Gilly's face. "It's distilled in the wilds of Scotland and smuggled into England through various rivers, such as the Tweed."

"I think they do an even greater business skirting the coast on the open sea," suggested George, very much interested in the subject.

"But is it so very difficult to stop them?" asked Francine in some surprise.

"I believe our scoundrels quite outnumber the preventive men," answered Taylor.

"How perfectly dreadful," decided Francine.

"Now cousin," said Charles quietly, "I do believe our own uncle has more than one bottle of Highland whisky in his cellar, and you can be certain he never paid a tax on them."

"And Gilly . . . you hold that smuggling goods and buying smuggled goods are one and the same crime?" asked Venetia quietly.

"Don't you, sis? I have often heard you deplore the buying of contraband as worse than the act of smuggling." He looked steadily into her dark green eyes.

"Well, yes, but . . ."

"Do excuse me, Miss Venetia," said Groomsby at her side, "but the squire has sent word that he is fully rested and would like the pleasure of yours and his nephews Westbourne and Iverness's company at once."

"Ah, a command performance," said Charles dryly. He stood up and bent to offer Venetia his arm.

She frowned and as she took it looked around. "Do please excuse us. I am certain Francine will manage to keep you all in line." With this and a smile, she allowed Charles to lead her off with Westbourne quietly, thoughtfully bringing up the rear.

"Why, do you think, has my uncle excluded my cousin Francine from this little gathering?" asked Charles provocatively, and then, "My God but you have the power to slay a man with a look! Do you know that, my dear?"

"No, I do not know any such thing." She smiled. "And do not think that I shall believe it just because you profess it to be so! You are very good at flattery."

"Fie on you, Venetia. Have faith in me, for in this instance, I am not lying." His voice dropped to a sensual cadence.

"Stap me if you aren't a knave, Charles!" snapped Westbourne on a harsh note before he was able to catch and curb his irritation. Having done this, he modified his tone and managed to pitch a chuckle into his next words. "Don't listen to him, Miss Tay, he doesn't know how to handle the truth!"

"And how very unflattering of you," teased Venetia, enjoying the banter immensely. She had the pleasure of finding herself flanked by both gentlemen as they made their way up the grand staircase to her uncle's room.

The squire sat thoughtfully in his bed. He was feeling stronger, and the hint of death had receded into a dark corner. Nevertheless, he meant to use its power to wield his might over these youths! They didn't know what was good for them, but he did, and by Jove, he meant to bring this thing he wanted about! A knock sounded on his door.

"Well, come in! Why in thunder do you think I sent for you? To stand out there? Nodcocks!"

Charles and Taylor exchanged glances of rueful amusement as Westbourne unlatched the squire's door for Venetia to pass through before them.

"Squire . . ." said Venetia pleasantly as she went to him and dropped a kiss on his forehead. She stood back and scanned his face. "You look very well this evening."

"Do I? Ha! Much you know," he grumbled and shook his head from side to side. "I'm going fast, and what is done about my wishes, eh? Naught!"

"Not so, Uncle," disclaimed Charles heartily. "I have been at pains to woo the lovely Miss Tay."

"Have you? Impudent toad-eater! But you aren't telling me anything. I know what goes on in m'own house!" He turned to Venetia. "And you, girl . . . do you mean to have him?"

Venetia frowned. "Squire, you know that I won't be swayed by your proposed will."

"And m'wishes? Won't that make a difference with you, girl? Eh? Thought you held me in some affection."

She released a short, lovely laugh and took his hand. "For shame. I don't mean to discuss this with you. You have issued your . . . orders. So be it." She turned to find that Charles had set a chair for her, and she smiled and took it.

The squire frowned at Iverness. "You . . . out! You might do better to court that empty-headed niece of mine downstairs!"

"But Uncle . . . I thought . . ." said Charles in some annoyance and surprise.

"Well, you thought wrong. Whatever you have been doing, it ain't been right, so out. I want a word with Venetia . . . and Westbourne."

Charles stiffened, made his uncle a bow and was closing the door at his back a moment later.

Venetia turned to the squire and said quietly, "That was not kind, squire."

"Eh? Does it matter to you how I treat that one?"

"It matters. He is, after all, in a precarious situation, and he is handling it as best he can."

The squire contemplated her a moment and then shifted his gaze to Westbourne. "And you? Do you mean to have Francine?"

"I think, Uncle, with all due respect, that whom I take for wife is my own business."

"Sauce-box! And you, minx . . . just the same! Go on, then . . . get out! But know this, Venetia. If you think I am being unkind to that nevvy of mine, think what you are doing if you refuse him . . . what Francine will do if she refuses him."

Venetia inclined her head. "No, squire, I cannot be manipulated. My life is my own. I don't have the power to manipulate another's with what I do. Yours is the hand that works here, not mine." With this she left him frowning darkly and made her way toward the door.

Westbourne took a moment to study her in some surprise and in much reluctant admiration before he started to follow. His uncle halted him.

"Taylor! Hold a moment . . . I would speak alone with you."

Chapter Twelve

*Venetia returned to her guests to find them con-*sorting with some freedom and a great deal of heat on the subject of Byron's latest submission to the English public. She had to smile to herself to see Francine sigh, "Oh, but *Don Juan* is so full of action . . . and he is ever so romantic. I can't help but think that like *Childe Harold*, Byron puts himself into the character he is portraying."

"Byron is a profligate and an exceptional cad!" snapped the good vicar.

George found Francine leaning into him and away from the vicar's harshness and immediately came to the poet's defense. "You are, I think, quite deceived by the all too publicized separation between Byron and his oh so good Lady Byron." George smiled ruefully over the memory of his poet friend's private remarks about his fateful marriage. "Byron is a lover of all life has to offer and probably his own worst enemy, but a cad? Never."

"No doubt he is good company for you!" returned the vicar, one brow up.

"Take care, vicar. Animadversions on myself I will allow, but not against a friend, and Byron is a friend."

The vicar, Venetia could see, was about to embroil himself in an argument better left unvoiced, and she quickly cut into the debate. "Come, I know what we can do," she said, drawing attention to herself as she moved across the room to a wall cabinet. "We can play at fox and hounds."

"But Van, that's a child's game," objected Ferdy.

"Oh, do let's play," cried Francine on a note of excitement. "It's ever so much fun."

George promptly agreed to it, as did the vicar after a moment's lecture on the frivolities of such activities. Venetia laid out the pieces for them before taking Ferdy aside.

"Now tell me, Ferdy, where have Iverness and Gilly gone to?"

"Iverness? Haven't the slightest idea. The last we saw of him he was off with you and Westbourne."

She raised one delicate brow. "Oh? And Gilly?"

Ferdy discovered the toe of his boot and frowned. "Well, as to that . . . I'm not m'friend's keeper, am I?"

"No, you are his friend and I am his sister and we both are worried about him. I saw it in your eyes tonight at dinner. Ferdy, he is involved in something . . . that could ruin him . . . ?"

Ferdy took her hand and squeezed it. "If I could stop him, I would, Venetia . . . you know that I would."

"Yes, dear, I know that you would. But . . ."

The door opened at their back and Westbourne stood in its hold. For some unknown reason, she discovered that her heart thumped guiltily, for her hand was still in Ferdy's grip and Westbourne's cold gray eyes had already perceived this fact. His dark brow moved and his lips curved ever so slightly into a sneer. He turned to the players on the floor. "Ah . . . what have we here?"

"Fox and hounds. Do you mean to join us, Taylor?" answered Francine happily.

Westbourne was silent a moment. "No, I think not." He made them a bow before he turned to take his leave of Venetia. "Goodnight, Miss Tay. I hope you may enjoy your . . . er . . . play."

"I am sure that I shall," she answered, her chin up, and why it was, she could not say. "But, my lord, are you off to bed already?" It was something she had not meant to ask. Why had she? Devil! Why did he force this absurd behavior out of her?

He smiled provocatively. "Perhaps." And his eyes told her exactly what he meant.

She felt the anger rise into a burning flame within her body, and it was all she could do to keep from retorting. Instead she turned and answered Francine's call to join them, for the game had started. She heard the click of the library doors, and somewhere inside of her, it jolted. Stop it! What did it matter where he went and what he did. She had nothing to do with him! Nothing!

Well, it was past midnight and Gilly had still not returned! There was nothing in that. After all, he was quite capable of staying out all the night, and she was certain that he had done so many times in the past without her even being aware. Why then was it so different this night? Because. Yes, because Gilly was playing deep, and she felt it in her bones that something was wrong, dangerously wrong.

That's what had prompted her into her breeches, sent her into her riding boots and her hooded cloak. That was the feeling as she hurried down the backstairs and let herself out into the cold chill of night air. The wind whipped at her face and blew away her hood.

Venetia took a moment to pull it around and low over her forehead as she made her way to the stables. The moon was full, and she could catch its glow glistening on the River Tweed below. And faith! What was that?

She stopped in her tracks as shadows on the water took shape and moved across the grassy beach. Dark forms vanished into trees, and Venetia bit her lip as she discovered she was staring at the hull of a sailing galley!

"What is this?" she said out loud but under her breath. She blinked. After all, night lights could play tricks on one. The squire allowed only one torch to burn all night, and that overlooked the front drive. She could go back for it. Perhaps she should, for its illumination did little for her at this distance. No, but then, whoever it was down there would definitely see her. Should she attempt to creep up on them and watch their activities undetected? She answered her own question by making a wild dart for the trees lining the open lawns that stretched out and down toward the river's enbankment.

As quietly as she was able she wound her way slowly, laboriously, until she heard the sound of guttural voices, several and all quite unfamiliar,

"The gaugers be making their way up the river to raid some of the stills in the North! Ha! They'll not find a one."

"Aye, and if the excise screws do find a still, it's to a Highland champion he'll have to answer!" laughed another in answer.

"Aye," agreed yet another in dangerous tones. "Let 'em try, it do 'elp a man's blood to be tipping them gaugers the double!"

"Hmmm," said the first, "did ye hear about Yawkins?" He laughed at the memory. "Did more than jest slided between those two cutters the other night. Lord, if he didn't hoist one of his casks as his maintop, threw his cap to one cutter, bowed to t'other and off he sails out of Manxman's Lake! Hell and firewater that Dutchman is made of!"

Was she having a dream? Had she floated into sleep or into a verse of Walter Scott's? What was this? Had all the talk of smuggling at dinner somehow warped her sense of understanding? Was she hearing incorrectly? Putting their words to her imagination? No. They were here on Ingram land . . . and the fact was they were unloading contraband. She could just see them, and they were unloading contra—

There her thoughts took an immediate halt and her blood chilled throughout her entire body. A voice rang out above all others because she recognized its familiar cadence.

"Stap me lads if you aren't a bunch of women!" Gilly laughed. "Do you mean to fatten your pockets by standing around blabbering about the Dutchman, or do you mean to hide his cargo?"

"Aw, now, young'un . . ." started one.

"Take care, Jester, what I lack in years, I've got in purpose," warned Gilly.

Gilly's voice! What was Gilly doing here . . . what was Gilly doing with smugglers? Oh, faith! No, it couldn't be Gilly! She peered around the trunk of the oak she had knelt behind. His fair hair blew unhampered in the wind, and though his profile looked stern, it was Gilly. Even in the dimness of the dusky light, she knew her brother.

"Well now, but we were jest 'aving a bit of fun, lad," returned the big man.

"So you were, but as I told you before, a cutter is due to pass here within the hour, and I want us well out of their way before then," snapped Gilly. He looked around warily, for he felt something, he didn't know what, but it was making him edgy. Perhaps it was being so near the house? Their last hiding place up the river had been discovered by the excisemen two days ago, so he had thought to use the underground cave he had discovered some years ago. Perhaps it wasn't such a famous idea after all.

"Aw, ye worrit aboot things sooo," scoffed another.

"That's why *I'm* in charge here!" riposted Gilly sharply. "My information is always accurate, and that's what has saved your necks until now. Be quick and step lively, for if we mean to get this cargo to the landsmen, it has to be concealed tonight."

Venetia backed away from the scene as though it were an awesome fire she had to get away from but could not quite believe. She tripped and fell, which tore away her hood, and as she got up a bramble caught her neck and scratched. She put her hand up to the wound with a wince and felt the blood ooze, but there was no thought of pain. There was only, Gilly? Gilly? What have you done? And why?

The ride from the Boar's Head in the village back to Ingram Place had seemed interminable. It was with considerable relief that Lord Westbourne saw the dark shadow of the stables down the long drive.

He had contrived to spend his evening free of Venetia! It had proved an impossible task. He allowed his tankard to be filled several times, hoping to drown her vision away, but there she had been, laughing, teasing, disapproving! What ailed him? What new vagary was this? He pulled a sardonic expression in the darkness. Yes, she was beautiful, and it wasn't the first time he had come across a beautiful woman. What was there about her that made his mind jump to her name, made him long to taste her lips, over and over?

He had to expunge her from his system. So why then didn't he just leave? His uncle had dared him to go . . . and that was another thing! What a damned strange interview that had been after Venetia had left them alone.

"Well, Taylor, what do you mean to do about that vixen of mine?" the squire had leveled at him.

"I don't think I understand your question, Uncle," he had returned cautiously.

The squire shook a finger at him. "I don't mean to get meself worked up, so don't you throw such fustian at me!"

"I am at quite a loss, though. I should never have referred to Francine as a vixen." He waited for the inevitable harangue and chided himself for baiting his uncle so unmercifully, at the same time thinking that the squire rather deserved it for attempting to control all their lives.

The squire, however, did not get angry. He did not splutter and he did not shout. Instead he leveled a penetrating stare at his favorite nephew's countenance and said slowly, "Put out with me, eh? Well, well . . . that is as it should be, but it won't matter in the end."

Westbourne frowned and sat on the edge of his uncle's bed and touched the withered man's hand. "Squire . . . Uncle . . . what you have set out to do—"

"Will be done," said the squire abruptly, firmly, and a smile curved his thin dry lips. "I don't mean to leave this world until that spitfire of my Gussie's has been seen to."

"You heard her—do you think she will take Charles?"

The squire started to retort and stopped short. "Don't you?"

At this, Westbourne again frowned. Truth was that if he believed what she had said earlier to the squire, no, then he did not believe she would have Charles. Why shouldn't he believe her? Because . . . just because she really had little choice. She might be balking at the forced circumstances, but in the end she would have to capitulate to fate. "No . . . I suppose you are right. She will have to surrender to your wishes in the end, and I suppose Charles will find himself more comfortable than he has been these past years. But Uncle, if you think I mean to—"

"Ha! I'm no fool." The squire shook his head. "I'm feeble of limb, my buck, but there are no maggots in m'head. You won't have Francine, and well I know it!"

"Then why—" started Westbourne in some surprise.

"No!" interrupted the squire, shaking his finger at him. "No, you answer me why, just why haven't you left here and gone back to London?"

Westbourne found himself at a loss. He did not want to reveal that he was not hanging out to be sure he was included in his uncle's will. Carefully, quietly and slowly he said, "But Uncle, I am here because you wrote and asked me to attend you."

"Yes, yes I did, but you are not dim-witted, lad, and you can see that I don't mean to put under just yet. So tell me, do you mean to remain here at Ingram Place until I finally croak?"

Westbourne laughed. "As a matter of fact, no, I don't, and more than that you are not going to get from me this evening."

"Then tell me . . . why are you staying? You aren't here for what you can get, or so you would have me believe. Why, Taylor, if not for that beauty of Gussie's?"

Westbourne made him a bow, formal and with a pinch of coolness, and as he came up said, "Because, dear Uncle, I wished to see you properly in form before I departed and left you to Charles!" With this he nodded and started for the door.

The squire did not mean to leave it at that. "Face it, lad, you've had your leveler!"

Westbourne directed one long sardonic look that silenced his uncle to dark grumblings, and as the squire watched the door close behind him, he snorted and pulled the covers to his chin. Damn, but he hoped he hadn't gone too far with Taylor, for the man had the look of a gentleman shocked into running.

The squire hadn't been too far from wrong, for that was exactly what his words had inspired in Westbourne. Hence his lordship's hasty flight from the house and his wild drinking in the tavern. He wasn't going to allow any fair-haired lovely to weave a spell around his head, and damn, why did her green eyes haunt him everywhere he went? Perhaps it was time he returned to London.

Taylor gave vent to his feelings with a sigh and dismounted heavily from his horse, steadied his wobbly limbs, for the drink still pounded in his head, and with a pat to the sleepy stableboy's shoulder he made his way toward the house.

Crashing through brush is a startling noise, especially when the ground is covered with dry leaves. Even in Westbourne's inebriated state he was immediately on guard as he turned toward the woods and called, "Who's there?"

There was no answer as Venetia picked herself up and attempted to find the path. Was that something, someone, at her back? Did she hear someone call? The wind took Westbourne's voice away and played tricks with the senses.

Westbourne charged stealthily forward and stopped short as a darkly clad form came tumbling breathlessly through a clump of evergreen bushes and tripped full into his arms!

Chapter Thirteen

Venetia's head was thrown back with the force of the impact. She gasped to then discover she was held in a steel-like grip. Thinking perhaps one of the smugglers had discovered her, she struggled for release.

Westbourne was astonished. What the devil was she doing running about in the woods at this hour? Why was she disheveled, and was this blood on her neck? "Venetia!" he said sharply.

She stopped at the sound of his voice. No smuggler here. This was Westbourne, and oddly enough she was flooded with relief. She sank into herself and against him. "Taylor . . ." It was a cry for help.

He heard it, and his gray eyes clouded over. Whatever had occurred had certainly upset her. "What is it, my love . . . what's wrong?"

She attempted to pull herself together. They had to get away from here. She couldn't tell Taylor her brother was a smuggler.

"Take me to the house, my lord, please."

"Of course," he said promptly, but instinct sent his glance around. What was she running from? With her neatly ensconced in his arm, he led her to the house and quietly within.

A dying fire still burned in the library grate. It was the only source of light in the cozy room, for Groomsby had snuffed all the candles earlier and had gone to his own quarters. Venetia was appreciative of the dark in her present circumstances and said nothing as Taylor poured her out a glass of brandy. He handed it to her almost abruptly in his impatience to discover what she was involved in at such an hour. He watched her take a sip, wrinkle her nose and start to set it aside.

"Finish it!" he commanded.

She didn't know why she found she could not refuse, but this was the case, and she did just that, in short distasteful sips. He waited all the while, took the glass from her and reset it on the tray. When he turned to her again, he was frowning. Her long white-gold hair was in a mass of disarray to her waist. Her cloak was loosely tied, and her tight breeches displayed to a fineness the perfection of form they concealed. Damnation but she was a beauty. He saw the dry blood on her neck and reached out to touch it.

"You scratched yourself."

"Did I?" She lowered her lashes, for she could not meet his eye. It was time to retire. It was time to take her leave. Why didn't she move? She had to get away from him, to think about this new . . .

He had her shoulders. "Venetia . . . what *is* going on?"

She couldn't meet his gray eyes. How could she? "I . . . I don't know what you mean," she answered lamely, ashamed as soon as the words were out.

He wanted to slap her. "Do you think I am a fool?"

She cut in sharply, "*No*, no I do not, nor do I trust you with my private affairs!" She bit her lip. "You . . . you have been very kind to me this evening, my lord, but what I do is really of no concern to you."

"Devil is in it that you should be right," he said on a hard note. The feel of her in his hands, the cherry lips so close, the green eyes so sad, so full with her need, drove him on with a sigh of resignation. "Ah, Venetia . . . you have cut up my peace." His mouth was on hers hungrily, passionately, and as he felt her respond, and she did, for she melted into his embrace willingly, he experienced a wild, most devastating sense of joy. His hand went to her face, and this time his kiss was gentle, tender, caressing, and when she pulled out of his hold, he allowed it.

She couldn't believe what was happening. Was she a brazen woman falling for this libertine? She looked up into his gray eyes and discovered desire. Yes, desire and something else that sent a shiver through her body. As bad as her brother? Was she a thrill seeker? Is that why she had refused to marry the vicar and those others that had come calling when her aunt had been alive? Was it because she wanted moments like this? Oh God, no! Without a word she ran from him, opening the library door wide and rushing the hall and the stairs to the darkness of her room. What was happening? Everything was going wrong!

Charles had seen Taylor enter the Boar's Head, but he hadn't the time to bother with his cousin, for he was being led abovestairs by as pretty a barmaid as he had seen in some days. No doubt, he thought, Taylor had come for the same pleasure, and it gave him a great deal of satisfaction to think he had beaten his cousin out with the fair maid.

When he descended the stairs to the tavern's galley, it was to find that Taylor had already left. It was early yet, and he was mildly surprised as he sipped his ale and wondered at it. Just what did Westbourne have in mind? He thought about the day. There was Taylor rushing off to secure a hack and drive the lovely Venetia home. Why had he done that if it was true that he wasn't after Venetia's hand? The more he thought about it, the more it disturbed him.

Tomorrow he would propose to Venetia and settle the matter. He sighed over it, for he wasn't really ready to throw away his bachelorhood, but there was nothing for it. The thing was it was either that or debtors' prison!

It was in this frame of mind that he made his way home. He was only slightly bosky from the night's entertainment and therefore it was with some alertness that he stopped at the peak of the drive and surveyed the river below. Was that a sound he had heard? And then coming up the long stretch of lawn was a familiar form whose youthful countenance could be perceived in the moonlight. Young Tay! Now, what the devil was Venetia's brother doing wandering about in the middle of the night?

"Gilly? That you, lad?" he called out in greeting.

Gilly stopped short in his tracks, and his mind went racing with answers to unspoken questions. "Hello . . . Charles, is it?" he returned in what he hoped was a merry tone.

"Of course it's Charles!" returned Iverness testily. "Don't say you took me for my cousin?"

"Oh no," answered Gilly unconsciously. "You two are not at all alike."

"Eh? Hmmm . . . well, yes, now come along with me to the stables," returned Charles, hopping off his uncle's horse, "and then we'll walk up to the house together."

"Right," answered the lad hesitantly.

"Right indeed!" Charles chuckled. "What bobbery have you been at? No good, I'd warrant."

Gilly pulled an excellent face, full with the secret of his doings, "Been having a round with the boys," he managed to say apologetically.

"Eh? And those boys, what, are they down at the river?" scoffed Charles on a note of disbelief.

"No, oh that . . . well, my sister has an uncomfortable habit of waiting up for me now and again. Thought I'd walk off some of my . . . er . . . better spirits."

Charles cast him a penetrating glance for a moment before accepting the youth's words. It

sounded odd to him. The lad was of age. What did
he mean by letting his sister interfere with his
pleasures? Well, well, so Venetia was capable of
keeping the boy on her apron strings? At any rate,
this was none of his affair. He might take a hand
to it, if it amused him after Venetia was his wife,
which brought him to the subject he wished to
pose to Gilly.

"Things might . . . could change for you in that
regard in the very near future, Gilly."

"Pardon, my lord," said Gilly, going formal.
"Change?"

" 'My lord' indeed. That is no way to address
your future brother-in-law. Wasn't I 'Charles' to
you just a moment ago?"

"Yes, well, sometimes I forget myself, but . . .
what do you mean, brother-in-law?"

"I plan to marry your sister," said Charles
gravely.

"Do you? Over Francine, you mean? Well . . ."
Gilly gave a short laugh. "I can't blame you for
that. Van is worth a thousand of Francine." He
shook his head. "You are out, though, if you think
she will have you."

"Really?" said Charles, drawing up to his full
height. "Why do you say so?"

"You are marrying because the squire gives you
no choice. Venetia won't let the squire dictate to
her. She would rather starve first."

"You are being melodramatic," snapped Charles.
"But . . . are you attempting to inform me that
your sister has an . . . aversion . . ."

Hastily Gilly cut him off. "Egad, no! In fact, I
think Van rather likes you. At least, she told me

she thought you were an engaging rascal, so I suppose . . ." He shrugged. "Look, I just wouldn't count on Van's having you."

"Gilly, I mean to have your sister, and all I want from you is a promise that if she should prove . . . reluctant, a promise that you might lend me your aid and sway her opinion."

Gilly snorted. "Impossible! You have met my sister. You have spent enough time in her company. Iverness, she knows her own mind. If you want her . . . well, I have no objection, but you'll have to win her on your own merit!"

They reached the stables, and the same young boy who had served as groom for Westbourne only minutes earlier came around disgruntledly and took charge of Iverness's horse. Charles ruffled the lad's mop of unkempt hair and turned to find Gilly appraising him. They fell into step beside one another as they took the remainder of the drive up to the house, and Charles pulled ponderously at his lower lip. There was more he wanted to broach to Gilly.

"It's that damnable will," he said slowly.

"Aye," agreed Gilly scathingly, "I'll grant you that. It's a damnable thing, all right, but it won't make a bit of difference to Venetia when she gives you her answer. If you mean to have her, you'll have to win her."

"And I have your blessing to go ahead and do that?" returned Charles.

Again Gilly considered the man. There was a charm about Charles that a youth like Gilly was drawn to, but even so, he wasn't sure that Charles was the sort of man to make his sister happy. "My blessing? Well, that's a might strong . . . but at least I have no objection."

They entered the house and moved across the hall to the stairs in the dim light, and Charles sighed. "And why not your blessing? What have I done that you would deny me that?" He didn't really care one way or another, for he meant to have Venetia, but he was momentarily diverted into curiosity.

Gilly continued up the stairs with Charles beside him, and he chose his words carefully. "My lord, no offense intended, for I did not mean that as a slur. It is just that . . . for all Venetia's level-headedness, she is, well, she has always dreamed of marrying someone who would . . . love her." They stopped at the landing, and Charles's brows drew together.

"And do you seriously think I would not love her?"

Gilly snorted. "Oh yes, and a hundred others as well."

Charles made no denial, though his brow went up. "Goodnight, Gilly."

"Goodnight, my lord," said Gilly softly as he watched the man turn and make for his quarters at the opposite end of the long corridor. Here was something new to consider, this very interesting development. Was it possible that Charles had fallen in love with Venetia? Why not? He wouldn't be the first. Well, but men like Charles just didn't fall into love easily. Men like Charles had been through the gamut of lovely women and their tastes were jaded, their hearts often warped, and

Gilly had seen nothing in Charles to prove otherwise.

He stretched and started for his own room. Would Venetia have him? He was different from the lads who had courted her during the days of Gussie's reign at Ingram. He was certainly a sight more romantic than the vicar. Just what would that difference mean to Venetia? Would her head be turned by Iverness's sophistication and experience?

It wasn't something he had control over, so he relegated it to the back of his mind and considered the evening's events. It had been a good night's work! Tomorrow night when it was feasible he would see the goods off on the Dutchman's schooner. Thank the Lord for Little Fanny. If it wasn't for the information she supplied about the revenue cutters they might have been caught long ago. Stupid excisemen. Easily outwitted when they spilled out their heads in bed with pretty Fanny. Dimwitted dolts, didn't they know she was ever faithful to her own kind? Didn't they know she was the Dutchman's pet?

Tomorrow night the Dutchman would sail his sloop down the Tweed through Berwick and hug the coast until he had dropped his cargo for his best profit. Profit? For his part in these activities, Gilly had been paid well. Soon, very soon, he would take Venetia to London and set her up in the style she deserved. It was an obsession with him.

The devil was in it that whenever he was touched by fear, by the chance of scandal, by the reality of what he was doing, he was excited. It turned his stomach sometimes to think he might be caught, but it thrilled him as nothing else ever had. What did he have to do all day at Ingram? Naught. So working toward this goal in the manner he had chanced upon some four months ago had become all-important.

Now here were Westbourne and Iverness upsetting things and getting a bit in the way. But never mind, Westbourne hadn't seen a thing, and Charles? No, Charles hadn't either. Venetia? Did she mean to have either of these men? No. She despised Westbourne. An odd thing, for after observing this man today he rather liked him. And Charles? No, he didn't think she would have Charles.

He opened his door and moved within laboriously, for he was just beginning to feel the weight of his weariness. A long heavy sigh escaped him as he pulled at his coat, and then a voice sailed through the air and nearly made him jump out of his skin.

"Tired, Gilly?"

Chapter Fourteen

It was Venetia. She was sitting on the bed like a statue, and he could just make out her form from the moonlight filtering in through the window.

"Van . . ." he managed to utter. "What the deuce?"

"Yes, of course you are tired," she said dully. "It is exhausting work, isn't it?"

"Work?" he returned warily. What was this? What was wrong?

"Oh, don't you think of it as work, Gilly?" She was angry, she was hurt, and the two emotions played havoc with her voice.

"Van, I don't know what you are talking about."

"Don't you, Gilly? I rather thought we didn't lie to one another. But then the definition of a lie to me has always meant deception. What has it meant to you, Gilly?"

"I don't lie to you, Van. There are things that are only my affair, not yours," he said defensively.

"Really? Then . . . is not my name Tay? If a scandal involves your name, Gilly, won't it touch me?" She hadn't meant to take this line of attack, but his behavior had drawn it from her.

"Van . . . tell me . . . tell me what you mean!" he demanded now. Could she know? How could she know? He was moving over to his branch of candles, taking out the tinder and lighting the three candles before he turned and saw that she was dressed in breeches, that her hair was a tumbling mass, and that there was dried blood beneath her cheek. "My faith! Van?"

"Do I have to do that, Gilly? Can't you find it in you to be honest with me now? Gilly . . . why?"

"Why?" he threw back at her. "Because I won't inherit in time to do right by you, Venetia! That's why! So I found another way!"

"Another way?" she returned incredulously. "You are a *smuggler*, for me?"

He softened his expression and reached out for her hand, as he sat beside her. "No sis, not for you, for me! I have been kicking my heels up here at Ingram, with naught to look forward to . . ."

She cut him off in agitation. "*Smuggling?* Gilly!"

"Van, we have enough, at least almost enough, to leave for London soon," he pleaded with her to understand.

"And what will you do there? Turn to the highway for your entertainment?" she returned fulminatingly.

"Van, you aren't looking at this as I am. How can you? You are a woman."

"What has that to do with anything?" she snapped. "Gilly, what have you become?"

"Bored! Bored to death with the life we lead up here. I don't have an estate to look after . . . at least, the trustees won't hand it over. I don't have anything to occupy my time. And sis, there were times before the squire's nephews came when I looked at you, at the old clothes you were forced to wear, and I wanted to die."

She touched his cheek. "Oh, Gilly . . ."

"I knew I couldn't remain here . . . but what to do? Smuggling? Yes, by God! I had the means to do it, for I met . . . someone who told me I could manage as middleman. And that's what I did!" He looked at her full. "I'm not ashamed, Van. I had no choice."

She took a full moment to compose herself. "Ethics played no part in your decision?"

"Ethics are intangible things. You were in rags, moving toward spinsterhood. That was a reality. I didn't know then that the squire was going to send for Westbourne and Iverness and throw them in your lap."

She put up her chin. "They don't change a thing," she stated.

"Right!" he agreed. "So they don't, and my initial plan to take you to London still stands."

"Absurd boy." She shook her head. "You won't do it any more, will you, Gilly?"

"I have one more shipment to see to, Van. And don't look like that. I gave my word, and the word of a gentleman is his bond. I can't withdraw. I won't withdraw."

"But Gilly . . ." she started.

"Go to bed, Van. All I can promise you is that after this next shipment, there'll be no more, because we two will be off for London."

"Gilly, you can't. Please . . . it's wrong and it's dangerous."

"You don't see at all, do you, Venetia?" he said in some impatience. "Well, there is no use trying to explain to you . . ."

"No use trying?" she cut him off. "Listen to yourself, you young halfling! Just listen to yourself. Think about what you have done and how you are excusing it!"

He took a turn about the room in a frenzy, his hands going through his hair. "Van . . . Van . . . I was going mad . . . I was, nearly, very nearly . . . so I started going out nights, drinking, from one tavern to another. Met these chaps, you know . . . and at first, well, it was a lark. But it served . . . you see, it served so easily . . ."

"Yes, I do see." She got up and went to him, touched his shoulder. "You shouldn't have stayed here at Ingram Place, kicking your heels and looking for something to do."

"Oh, a paltry fellow you think me!" he scoffed. "What? Should I go off to London and leave you? Not I!"

She sighed heavily. "Go to bed, dearest . . . I can see you are quite done in. But Gilly, we'll have to talk more about this."

He dropped a kiss on her forehead and led her to

the door. "No, no, I don't think we will, Van. It is nearly over, you know. Just one more run."

"Oh, Gilly . . ." she started but cut herself off. She had to stop him, but how? She would retire to her own room and think this out. Perhaps she could take him away? She would have to do something, but what? Just what could she do?

Vicar John Qerkdon had decided to assert himself. He wanted Venetia to be his wife, and thus far he had not been successful in persuading her to agree. He had given the matter much thought and had decided that females were a romantic bunch and that more than likely he had gone about the matter too lamely. What was needed here was a little forcefulness. What was needed was some aggression. The thought of such action immediately put him to the blush and rather excited him all at once.

It was in such a mood that he arrived at Ingram Place and sought Venetia out. As it happened she was already up and about, for she had not spent a peaceful night. She was in a sad state of nerves and had avoided meeting anyone at breakfast by leaving through the rear door of the house and seeking the orchards as a place to walk off some of her irritation.

Upon being informed that Groomsby was sure he didn't know where Miss Venetia had taken herself off to, the vicar delivered a severe lecture to the butler and decided to search out his love himself. By chance a movement in the toolshed caught his attention, and he took that direction, which led him to the back of the garden. There he stood and took stock of his surroundings and discovered a wisp of yellow as Venetia meandered down the apple-tree-lined path.

He put up his hand. "Venetia," he called and brought her progress to a halt.

She looked up to find him bowling down upon her and sighed. "Hello, John."

She was stunning! It was his first discernible thought as he stood and looked. He couldn't remember having ever seen her look so beautiful. (An odd thing, as Venetia was not at that moment looking her best.) He took a step forward and gulped. She wore no bonnet, and her long hair was tied at the nape of her neck with a yellow ribbon. She wore a dark-brown spencer over her yellow day gown, and her green eyes were remarkable for their depths. She would make him the perfect minister's wife. This was his second discernible thought, and he discovered that her gloved hand was delicate and small as he pulled her forward and into his arms.

"Venetia!" he said dramatically before he pressed his lips to hers.

She was so startled that she did not at first resist. However, as he gave every indication of pursuing this course she managed to put up her hand. "John! Stop it! Behave yourself!" And then in some exasperation, for he had begun to press his kisses around her face, *"John!"*

The breakfast parlor was a cozy room filled with exotic blooms. They had been a passion with the squire's wife, and he maintained them in her memory. Seated around the table were Francine,

Iverness and Westbourne when Groomsby arrived with the information that Mr. Whitney was desirous of paying a morning call on Miss Fenton.

Francine blushed brightly and mumbled something about Mr. Whitney's being unfashionably early.

Iverness's eyes darted to Westbourne and he said slowly, almost insidiously, "Why, Francine, you don't mean to send the poor boy away?" he turned to his cousin, Taylor. "Don't you think we should invite Mr. Whitney to breakfast with us?"

"Indeed I do!" agreed Westbourne promptly. "Groomsby, have Mr. Whitney join us here." Then in an undervoice to Iverness, "You misread the cards, old boy."

"Do I?" said Iverness thoughtfully. Well, well, then perhaps Westbourne meant to have not Francine, but Venetia? He was going to have to work quickly to snip this.

Whitney came into the room in a flourish of great looks and gallant manners, and it wasn't long before Francine's lashes were brushing her cheeks and George was whispering into her ear. Charles pushed away his plate and looked toward the door. Where was Venetia? Gilly too had not come down to breakfast. As this troubled him, he decided to ring for Groomsby and inquire after her.

Westbourne had risen from the table and moved to the window. It was a bowed structure in the fashion of the heyday of the Regency and overlooked the orchards. He was just in time to see the vicar scoop Venetia wildly into his arms.

Westbourne's feelings went into a violent state

of heat. He found himself gripping the drape with some force and released it viciously before he was able to collect himself. He took to pacing but could not draw his glance away from the pair at the end of the orchard path. It was then that he observed Venetia's struggle to be free. He didn't need more. Without a word, without knowing why, without thinking, he was excusing himself in some rush and leaving the room to nearly run down the back corridor that led to the rear door and his destination.

Charles watched Westbourne's departure between knit brows. His inclination was to follow, but he had sent Groomsby in search of Venetia and meant to await her arrival. He looked across at the two youngsters whispering nonsense at each other and felt irritated by it all. Just what the devil was going on?

In the meantime, Westbourne had put ground behind him and had reached the vicar's shoulder just as Venetia had squealed with annoyance and exasperation at the vicar's relentlessness, *"John!"* She did not see Westbourne's descent as she attempted to yank out of the impassioned vicar's hold. "Do stop . . . please, John!"

He might have listened at this point; however, he did not have the opportunity to do so, for he was mightily held in a steel grip and spun around to receive a hammerlike right fist in his belly. The vicar groaned, Venetia screamed, and Westbourne brought up his left to the vicar's bonebox.

The vicar went reeling but was fortunately prevented from falling by the apple tree at his back. Venetia screeched with some agitation as she went to him, "John, oh you poor dear . . . are you hurt?"

The vicar looked at his attacker in some consternation and realized that had Westbourne meant to hurt him, he would now be in a great deal of pain. He noted Venetia's ready sympathy and decided to utilize it as he tested his jaw with an expressive groan.

"It isn't broken," offered Venetia helpfully.

"No thanks to you, my lord!" snapped the vicar, his eyes glaring at Westbourne. "Tell me, Venetia, are the men in your uncle's household all mad?"

Something in the situation suddenly caught Venetia's sense of the ridiculous and she wanted to giggle. She managed to restrain herself and said as evenly as she could, "Well, but John . . . this time, you rather did provoke the attack. After all . . ."

The vicar pulled himself up to his full height and looked down at Venetia with hurt pride filling his vague eyes. "*You* think that? You stand here and defend this . . . this . . . sneaking knave?"

"Tread warily, sir," warned Westbourne. "Unless, of course, you mean to defend your words."

The vicar rounded on him. "I am, my lord, in case you have not noticed, a man of the cloth!"

"And were you a man of the cloth when you forced your attentions on Miss Tay?" retorted Westbourne, once again feeling his ire stirred.

"Stop it! Both of you." She turned to the vicar. "I am sorry, John, but I think you had better go."

The vicar made her a stiff bow. It would seem that he would have to look elsewhere for a wife. This had been borne in on him thoroughly. More dramatically than sadly he said, "Goodbye, Miss Tay."

She did laugh then and touch his arm. "Nonsense, John, only good day."

He was held in check by her green eyes full with their mischief. She was a friend. She had been a friend for years, and she would always be that. He sighed and patted her hand. "True, all too true, Venetia."

She stood and watched him leave before she was able to turn and face Westbourne. "Well, you've done a day's work, haven't you?"

"I wouldn't have had to if you hadn't led the poor man on!" he snapped. He was feeling a spot of pity for the vicar.

"Oh, now that is too much! You come charging in like a bull, but put the blame on me? Isn't that just like you!"

"Doesn't that blame belong with you? He has been left to you for some time. You could have convinced him that you weren't interested, but you didn't because you were playing out your cards! Isn't that true, Venetia?" He had her shoulders.

"You devil! How dare you! And no, my lord, no, that isn't true!" returned the lady hotly.

Chapter Fifteen

"So here you are!" It was Charles coming up on them speedily. He had observed the vicar's stony departure and had hurried along in time to see Westbourne and Venetia in something of a passion. An angry passion to be sure, but a passion all the same, and to Iverness's way of thinking, this was dangerous. "Come on, then, Venetia, for I have had the staff keep the coffee hot for you."

Venetia wasn't sure she was happy for the interruption. There was still a great deal more she wanted to say to Westbourne, but she turned to Charles and suddenly could not control herself. She wanted to flirt with Charles because she wanted to get to Westbourne and teach him a lesson! So he thought she had led the vicar on? So he thought she had dallied with John, eh? Well, she would show him what dallying meant, and she would show him with someone who knew the rules of the game! She glided toward Charles and took his arm. Her eyes invited as she looked up into his attractive face. "Charles, what a gallant you are! I am famished, so you may take me right back and ply me with coffee!" She was, of course, behaving outrageously, but at that moment she didn't give a fig!

Charles fell right in step with her sport and said caressingly, "If I ply you with coffee, will you reward me?"

She laughed lightly and rapped his hand gently. "Cad! You are taking advantage of a hungry lady!"

"I hope so," he said on a lower note and turned to smile victoriously at his cousin as he bore her away.

Westbourne looked after them in something of a mild fury before he was able to check himself. A frown descended with his thoughts, and his thoughts turned into questions. There were many questions that had answers that did not fit with what he had previously believed to be the situation here at Ingram Place. What to do? Damn if he was going to let Charles use Venetia to gain his inheritance! As soon as this thought intruded he banished it brutally. What the deuce did it matter to him? It didn't. If they wanted one another, if they wanted to make a marriage of convenience, what the devil did he care? Fiend seize it! He did!

"You know, Venetia, that I am quickly growing fond of the notion of being your husband," Iverness said softly as he led her down the hall to the breakfast room.

She laughed in her way and then arched a brow at him. "And that announcement should, I take it, send me into transports?"

He eyed her and said carefully, for he was aware she was teasing, but not sure how far away from the tease he could take her, "Venetia, you would not want me to lie, to admit an emotion I haven't had the time to explore?"

"Oh no, my lord," she said demurely, and this time a great deal in earnest, "so let us be reasonable—do not expect me to react to your lovemaking with any feeling."

He read the hit in her green eyes and was momentarily taken aback with the sudden impact of their force. It occurred to him that given the time he could grow accustomed to life with this one. "*Touché,* my dear, and do you know that more and more I really do believe our alliance may be the making of me."

"Do you? But you take for granted what has not yet been agreed to," she cautioned on a graver note.

"Venetia, we need one another . . . and I think for a start, that is not so very bad." He had her shoulders. "Stap me, child, but I think we may deal together."

"Yes," she said seriously, "I agree with you, Charles . . . I think we might get on famously together, and for some that might be enough . . . for some . . ." Her trailing voice softened but stopped as she found Charles looking past her to

someone else. She turned and discovered Westbourne standing.

Westbourne's eyes were full of contempt, and
his voice matched the sneer that had curved his
lips. His words, his look, were for her alone, "My,
you are having a busy morning."

Charles took an angry step forward, Venetia
held his arm, Groomsby appeared around the bend
of the hall and cleared his throat, and once again
Venetia was struck with a giddy feeling that
made her want to giggle.

"Miss Venetia," said Groomsby apologetically,
"there is someone in the drawing room ... I
think ... if you will forgive me, that you must
see."

"Well, there you are, Charles, but I think it
must be the young Ferdy trying to steal a march
on you," said Westbourne dryly.

Venetia sighed and attempted to ignore Westbourne. "Groomsby, if it is Ferdy, do tell him—"

The old butler cut in on her, "Excuse me, miss,
but it isn't Ferdy," he said meaningfully, his eyes
lingering on hers.

She frowned. "No? Well then, who?"

"Heigh-ho, Charles!" continued Westbourne
loudly. "Yet another suitor to contend with! Just
what will you do?"

Charles glared a dagger at him. "Why, cut them
out ... all of them."

Venetia rounded on Westbourne. "Stop it! Just
stop it." Then, because she was out of temper, she
turned on Groomsby. "Well, why don't you tell me
who it is?"

"Yes, of course, miss," said Groomsby. "He gave

his name as Preventive Officer Crail." Clearly the retainer was unhappy about having to expose this piece of information before Westbourne and Iverness.

"Preventive ... but ... what. . . ?" stammered Venetia, caught with a sudden fear. She exchanged glances with Groomsby. What did the butler know? How much did he know? What was an exciseman doing here? "Yes, of course. I shall see him at once."

"Thank you, miss. I told him, you see, that the squire was not well enough to grant him an interview."

Was Groomsby conveying a message to her? Oh, faith! What was she going to do? "Thank you, Groomsby. Would you have a tray of coffee brought to us in the drawing room, please." She turned first to Iverness. "I shall see you later, my lord." To Westbourne she only nodded, and then she was moving swiftly and with a trembling heart to the drawing room.

Iverness was frowning. A preventive officer here at Ingram Place? Why? He looked up and found Westbourne thoughtfully watching Venetia's retreat. And that was another thing. Did Westbourne want Venetia?

"Look here, Taylor ... if you are not careful, Francine will take young Whitney."

"I hope that she may, for the old boy is driving me mad with his suspicions, and the sooner the better, for if ever a pair were made for one another . . ."

It occurred to Charles that he had thought very much the same thing after observing the silly couple, but he sighed. "You are doing yourself out of a hefty inheritance, though. Doesn't it gall?" He was curious.

Westbourne relented. It wasn't fair, after all, for Charles really did have to marry to save himself. "Look, Charles . . . to be honest, no, it doesn't because—"

"Oh, I see what it is," snapped Charles, cutting in sharply. "It is Venetia! You mean to have her, do you? Well, I can't say that I blame you for throwing your cap that way, but it won't serve. She don't like you."

"Doesn't she?" Westbourne's back was up. "What makes you think I care?" Forgotten was his earlier resolve to trust his cousin with the confidence of his financial status.

"Care? By Jove, man, just look at you! I'd swear you're half daft with wanting her. Has you up in the boughs and walking a tightrope. Too bad, cuz . . . for it's me she'll take in the end."

"Do you think so? Well, well . . . perhaps you have presented me with a challenge, Charles, and you know I have ever been one to take on a difficult task!"

Charles stood alone in the hall and watched his cousin saunter off with a feeling of regret. He had definitely gone too far. Damn, he had mishandled the situation. Until now his cousin had not actively sought Venetia's hand. Then his mind flew to the fact that a preventive officer was now closeted with Venetia. What the deuce was going on?

* * *

Preventive Officer Crail was a man who had seen the better side of forty and a man who was disillusioned with the people in the North that dared to call themselves English subjects. Smugglers they were, all of them, whether they were actively engaged or just looking the other way. Fed up he was, and tired of fighting a losing battle. Well, now here was a pretty thing, what with the gentry throwing in with the free-traders! A pretty thing indeed, and that was what had brought him to Ingram Place, an honest piece of information that Mr. Gilly Tay had been doing just that.

Venetia came into the room, hand extended, white-gold hair perfectly framing her lovely face, and the exciseman was taken off his guard, for her natural elegance immediately intimidated him.

"Good morning, Officer Crail. I am Miss Venetia Tay." She indicated a chair, after she had allowed him to gently shake her hand. "Won't you sit down?"

He couldn't, wouldn't allow the fact that she was a beautiful woman to sway him. Her brother was in serious trouble, and so he would have her know. "No, no, I don't think the nature of me visit calls for it."

"Oh?" she said, one brow lifted. She felt a moment's shame as she knew she was about to put on a haughty air, "Well then, sir, I do hope you won't mind if I sit down?"

"Of course," he shot off quickly and took a step forward.

Venetia took her time, sat, positioned her muslin skirt, sighed and then smiled as she looked at him full. She meant to put him off as much as she could and was using her instincts, "Well then, sir, what can I do for you?"

"Er ... I ... er ... well then, you know, of course, that I am ... a preventive officer."

"Of course." She nodded gravely. "And it is a wonderful thing you and your men do in our parts."

"Yes, yes, it is not that we get any thanks for it, nor do we want any thanks, but when we get stabbed in the back for our troubles ... well then, 'tis a sorry state of affairs, let me tell you!"

"Oh dear ... what can you mean?" returned Venetia.

Treasure of treasure, had he found a sympathetic ear? He dove right in. "Do ye know what we are up against? Did ye know that even the farmers 'elp these flaskers along?" He shook his head. "No, what would a gently bred maid be knowing of sech things?"

"I don't understand. Do you mean we actually have smugglers in our own area? Why ... where do they come from?"

"Scotland! Aye, they distill in the Highlands and run the whisky to England, they do ... wit' the 'elp of Englishmen!"

"Oh my ... and what a job it must be for you to stop them."

"It is that! Why just the other night, we sent one of our lads out on the information that their landsmen were taking a wagonload of whisky down a ... er ... a certain pike, not far from here as a matter of fact. Our officer stopped the cart and challenged the two scoundrels."

"Faith, sir, what happened?"

"They dared to lay hand to an officer of the king! They trussed him up and laid him in the middle of the road!"

"Upon my soul! The poor man ... he could have been killed by some odd traveler in the dark."

"Aye, so he told them ... and they up and dumped 'im at the road's edge. Had a good laugh over it, they did. It's a wonder they didn't break the young'un's spirit!"

"What can we do? This is simply awful. But I don't understand what it has to do with us at Ingram Place," said Venetia gently, thinking it time to bring matters to a head.

He eyed her for a long moment. "Well, Miss Tay ... I won't arglebargle wit ye over this. Fact is, we 'ave it on excellent authority that the section of the river that cuts through Ingram Land has been used for the purpose of ... well ... thing is ..." He found it strangely difficult to meet her eye and pounce on her with his accusation.

"Yes?" she urged.

He retracted slightly. It could be dangerous throwing unsubstantiated charges at the nobility's heads. His superiors could have his own, in fact, if nothing proved out. "I am sorry to 'ave to tell you that we 'ave reason to believe ... with or without your brother's knowledge ... that Ingram land was used for the illegal purpose of whisky running." There, it was out. He turned beet-red, for the lady jumped to her feet with indignation.

Groomsby entered with the coffee tray and set it

down. She waited for the retainer to leave them alone and gave the appearance of a woman composing herself and her reply. Her hands folded at her lap. "Your information is incorrect, Officer Crail. My brother would certainly know if anyone were to try such a thing and he would have immediately notified the Preventive Station!"

"Would he have?"

"I don't appreciate that question and won't dignify it with an answer. In fact, sir, I think we have nothing more to say to one another."

"Don't we?" He couldn't take it any further. He didn't have enough to back himself up. "Then . . . perhaps I should speak with Mr. Tay. I thought perhaps I would speak with you or the squire first and see if there might be anything I could learn . . . to help us with our cause for the king and country. I see I was mistaken."

"How dare you! I think, Officer Crail, you have overstayed your welcome." She moved toward the door and thought to add as she opened it, "I will, however, be sure to advise my brother of your visit and your conversation. Perhaps he might not be outraged, as I am, but amused. Good day to you, sir."

There was nothing more he could say. Hat still under his arm, he stiffly made her his bow and departed, leaving Venetia to pace. A few moments later she went in search of her brother.

Chapter Sixteen

"Hold there a moment," called Charles of Iverness as he hurried out of the house after the brightly clad dragoon officer.

Preventive Officer Crail turned and with knit brows waited for Charles to approach. He was not pleased with the results of his visit to Ingram Place. He was no closer to his quarry, and if anything, it would only serve to warn off young Tay. His mood was as a result gravely affected as he awaited the well-dressed gentleman hounding him down.

"Allow me to introduce myself sir," said Charles, slightly breathless. "I am the squire's nephew, Lord Iverness, and it has come to my attention that you wished an audience with my uncle."

"Well, yes . . . but his man said that he is not well enough."

"Very true. Officer Crail, isn't it?" He waited for the dragoon's nod. "Yes. Shall we walk along to the stable and chat?" He waited for the dragoon to fall in step with him. "Groomsby did quite right by showing you into the drawing room and having Miss Tay meet with you, for I was closeted with my uncle at the time. However, I am certain that you would much rather discuss your business with someone . . . shall we say . . . in a better position to aid you?" He had no idea why the dragoon was here at Ingram Place, but he meant to find out. Instinct told him to find out.

Officer Crail unabashedly looked Charles over from head to foot. Here was a gentleman, clothed perhaps for the London set he would put down as dandified. Information had it that the squire's nephews had only just arrived at Ingram Place. What could he do? Naught, and confiding in him, well, that might stir up more dust. Careful now, Crail told himself. "As to that, Miss Tay answered my questions readily enough."

"Did she? Excellent. So then you leave Ingram Place fully satisfied," returned Charles at his most charming.

"Well now, I wouldn't be saying that. . . . Look here, m'lord, there is free-trading going on and I wouldn't be satisfied till it's stopped!"

"Free-trading, you say? Smuggling? By Jove, man . . . near Ingram Place?" returned Charles, feeling a swell of excitement. Was there something here he could use?

"You ask me and I'll answer you, but bring another into it and I'll deny it, for I mean to keep my place."

"In confidence, man, what are your suspicions? You have nothing to fear from me. I want Ingram Place safe."

"Aye. Well, then, you might want to keep a watch, for we think your uncle's land has been used for storing contraband. Whot's more . . . but never mind that. I've said enough, and unless you can offer me some information on the matter, I'll be taking me leave of ye."

They had reached the stable doors, and Charles stopped abruptly. Smuggling here at Ingram Place? Contraband here at Ingram Place? How? Who? It wasn't possible. He held the dragoon's arm. "What makes you think such an absurd thing?"

"Naught that Miss Tay gave me, I'll tell you that. But we got our reasons to think it so."

Charles stood aside and allowed the officer to pass into the stable. It was then that he caught Westbourne's eye. Blister it! Had Westbourne heard them talking? How much had he heard? Why the deuce it mattered he couldn't at that moment understand. He only knew that it did.

Taylor grinned and aside to his cousin he said quietly, "Eh, Charles, taking up the life of a free-trader?"

"Go to the devil!" returned Charles testily.

"So I shall, but not just yet." Westbourne nodded to the dragoon as the man passed and waited until the officer was mounted and well on his way down the driveway. "In the meantime, tell me, Charles, isn't that a bit risky here at Ingram Place?"

"Fiend seize you, Taylor! Do you think I am such a twiddle-poop? Don't answer that! And no, I may be many things, but I thank you I haven't stooped quite that low yet."

Westbourne shrugged his shoulders. "Why the preventive officer here at Ingram Place?"

"Why indeed!" snapped Charles meaningfully. "And what have you been doing here in the dark of the night, Taylor?"

"Sleeping, Charles . . . and dreaming of the fair Venetia. What else could I do here at Ingram Place?" With this he had led his horse out the stable door and mounted.

"Well, that is all you will do about her . . . and I wonder at you now, leaving her to me. Thank you, Taylor!"

"No, don't thank me, Charles . . . for I have a fancy to cut you out with her, and you will need more than this afternoon to win the lovely, depend upon it!" With this Westbourne sent his steed into a collected canter down the drive, leaving his cousin to ponder darkly at his back.

Why he had egged Taylor on was more than he could fathom. His cousin seemed always to have that effect on him. They had never been able to deal well together. There was too much competition and not enough esteem. But that was something else, and not the problem right now.

What did the dragoon mean? Free-trading at Ingram Place? Right under his uncle's nose? Well, the squire was ill . . . what would he know? But Venetia . . . she would know? Good God! Could Venetia be involved in such goings-on? No. It was impossible. But . . . hold a moment. What of young Tay? Yes, by faith! What if Tay had embroiled himself in such a lark? Venetia! Where was she now? He would go and search her out, for by all that was sacred, he meant to make Westbourne eat his words! Ha! Taylor and Venetia? Ha, she disliked Taylor . . . didn't she? A sudden doubt took hold of him and sent him nearly racing back toward the house and his intended bride.

Venetia had in the meantime ascertained that Gilly had left the house in the early-morning hours and that Groomsby had no idea where he was, though he was gravely concerned. She studied Groomsby's countenance and listened to the tone of his words and decided that the faithful retainer had his suspicions. Never mind, she could trust him. But where to go?

Ferdy? Had Ferdy known all this time and allowed Gilly to proceed with his precarious and illicit trysting? Would he help her to persuade Gilly to cut off his connections with the smugglers? She had no answer to this, but of one thing she was certain: Ferdy would know where to find Gilly, and Ferdy would help her to warn him about this evening. Gilly might this very moment be setting up the night's schemes. She had to hurry, but this was a thing that posed a problem.

The Honorable Ferdy Skillington had taken up bachelor's lodgings in Cornhill on the Tweed when he discovered that he needed to get away from his parents' meddling in his affairs. His future plans were to move to London for the Season, but for now his quarters could be found in a neat lodging house in the quaint village of Cornhill. However, these same lodgings were definitely *not* open to gently bred females who wished to retain their good reputations.

Venetia's sense of propriety was often informal, but never had she crossed the fine line. This would be definitely crossing the line. What to do? She had to get a warning to her brother, and at that moment Ferdy was the only one she could trust to handle the situation. She could perhaps find a linkboy to fetch Ferdy outdoors to meet her. Yes, the venture need not be as hazardous as she had at first believed.

Hopeful, she quickly changed into her new emerald-green velvet riding habit with its matching top hat, and adjusted the hat so that its white silk banded bow flanked her well-shaped head at a jaunty angle. She pulled her comfortable riding boots on and rushed down the backstairs to the ground floor, where she hurried to the house's side door, grateful that she had not been observed.

She opened the door and peeped out to find Charles coming up the drive from the stables on foot, evidently returning to the house. She scurried behind a large evergreen bush and waited until she was sure he had reentered the house before she dared another look. No one there. Good! She darted across the lawns and made her way breathlessly to the stable, hoping her mare had not yet been turned out.

An inquiry there brought a sheepish groom out with an excuse about having been too busy to turn the mare out, what with his having had the dragoon's horse to attend to and then Westbourne's horse.

"Oh, then Lord Westbourne has ridden out?" she asked.

"Aye, that he has ... some twenty minutes ago, miss."

"Did he say where he might be going?"

"No, miss."

"Right, then, I shan't be more than two hours ... and if the squire sends for me, you may send word that I have gone into the village on an errand." With this she was mounted and urging her horse off into a jog down the long driveway that led to the main pike. She was in a state of nervousness, for she wanted to get to Gilly, but she didn't wish to draw attention to herself by cantering off to Cornhill and stirring up a dust behind her.

Westbourne reached the village of Cornhill on Tweed and stopped one pedestrian and then another until he was put on the right route, for he had a specific destination in mind. As it happened he made the correct turn and passed through the quaintly styled shops and village cottages to a small, official-looking building just outside the town. Its signpost labeled it as a Preventive Station and its occupants were unused to visitors, but it was there that Lord Westbourne dismounted and tethered his horse, loosened the animal's saddle girth and made his way within.

The interior of the small building housed a black cast-iron stove that nicely warmed the very nearly empty chamber. A large orderly desk commanded the center of the room, and the walls were well armed with many weapons of various sizes and uses. Behind the desk sat a lieutenant of pleasant countenance and average size who looked up inquiringly as Westbourne entered.

A quick survey of the visitor's person excited such an interest that the young lieutenant jumped from his chair, overturned it without a backward glance and charged at Westbourne with some boyish glee. "Famous! *You* . . . here? I can't believe it! Damn, but it's good to see you, Taylor!"

Westbourne responded in kind, and there was some back-slapping and warm greeting before the young lieutenant pulled out a chair and shoved it at his lordship and sat on a corner of his desk.

"How the devil did you know I was here? Who could have told you? I'd swear no one knew it yet. Good God, I've only been here a week."

"Hold on, lad. I had no idea you were here."

"What? You must be bamming me. You walk in free as you please into a Preventive Station and tell me you aren't here to see *me!* The devil you say! What the deuce did you come for, if not for me?"

"Puffed up! Should have let you go a couple of rounds with those bruisers. Would have put you down a bit, and from the looks of it, you need to come down a peg, Thomas lad." The two had met one evening in London when the young Lieutenant Thomas Burford had been set upon by a pack of ruffians out for mischief and blood. Back to back they had taken the group on and had been fast friends ever since.

"Thought that was what you did do." The lieutenant grinned.

"Careful . . . I might have a go at you myself."
Westbourne smiled easily.

"But seriously, Taylor, what are you doing here,
then?"

"At your Preventive Station? And what the
bloody hell are you doing in a Preventive Station?"

"Relieving a friend of mine. He took on another
post, and I wanted out of London for a time.
Remember that pretty little bit of muslin that
caught my eye in Pall Mall that night we were on
our way to Worth's for dinner?"

"So I do. You caught up with her, as I remember
. . . you never made it to Worth's." Westbourne's
grin was wide.

"Aye . . . fine little bird. But we had different
ends in mind. Thought I'd cut it short . . . so here
I am."

"Hmmm. Here you are," said Westbourne, ready
now to bring matters to the heart of his visit.

"Yes, but what are you doing in Northumberland?" returned Thomas.

"My uncle is ill . . . sent for me." Westbourne
was frowning. "You may have some memory of
my mentioning him? Squire Ingram?"

"Good God! The squire is your uncle?" returned
Thomas in some surprise.

"Yes. Does that take you aback? Why, Thomas?"

The young lieutenant flushed. "No reason."

"Thomas, I never thought you would try to pitch
gammon at me," said Taylor, half in earnest, half
teasing. "It won't serve, you know."

"No? Well, I suppose not. Then you know my
man was up to see your uncle this morning?" He

shook his head. "Can't imagine where Crail is . . . he should have returned."

"I don't fancy he learned much at Ingram Place. Perhaps he is following up with another lead," suggested Westbourne, fishing for information.

The lieutenant got up from the corner of his desk, went around it and sat at his desk chair, keeping the desk between him and Westbourne.

"I am afraid I cannot discuss this matter with you, Taylor." His tone was grave, official.

Westbourne gave a low whistle. "Serious, is it? How is it then that your dragoon accepted to discuss the matter with Miss Tay?"

"What?" Thomas jumped up from his chair. "He did what?"

"Now what is this?" asked Westbourne, surprised. Had he hit a soft spot? Why? Just what was all this about? That was what he had come to discover. His confrontation with Charles earlier had been just that; he hadn't thought for a moment that Charles was embroiled in smuggling. But why the tender spot regarding Venetia? He felt a trickle of fear. "I tell you that when my uncle was not well enough to see your dragoon, he was taken in to Miss Tay. Odd, considering the fact that he should have seen either myself or my cousin Lord Iverness, but there you have it, and I should like to know why a dragoon was up at Ingram Place."

"I am saddled with fools up here, do you know that, Taylor? Dear faith! How he can have accepted to see . . . but never mind, 'tis done!"

"Thomas, I think that I shall ring your all too

thin neck in a moment!" He got to his feet. "What was a dragoon doing at Ingram Place?"

Thomas sat down and considered his friend for a long moment. "It is a most delicate matter. The ᶠact that your uncle's man took my officer in to see Miss Tay—not you, not your cousin—indicates that even the Ingram butler must be in on this affair."

"Now Thomas, I will know what the hell you are talking about!" snapped Westbourne, more than understandably upset. If Venetia was involved, so was he. A fact that had no logical reason or bearing, but a fact and one that he meant to think about, but not now. Now he had to extricate Venetia from trouble, for he had a very strong feeling that she was in trouble. . . .

Chapter Seventeen

*Unaware of Westbourne's activities, though a fleet-*ing thought of him touched her mind more than she thought understandable, Venetia made her way to Cornhill on Tweed and sought out Ferdy's lodgings. She had a vague notion where this might be, and it didn't take her long to point her horse in the correct direction.

Outside his building no linkboy could be found, and she stood, her horse's reins in her hands, her delicate brows drawn together in some doubt as she tried to decide what she could do. There was nothing for it. She would have to go back to the village stables and have her horse seen to while she visited with Ferdy. Her mare attended to, some moments later found Venetia taking the steps to Ferdy's door.

A knock brought forth a pudgy-faced undersized gentleman's gentleman who looked shocked at Venetia. She attempted to ignore his expression and said as though it were the most natural thing in the world, "Would you please call Mr. Skillington to attend me?" She stepped within and stood just inside the narrow hall.

The retainer closed the door, "Mr. Skillington is getting dressed."

"Is he? Good, then tell him I await him . . . please," said Venetia cheerily.

"Very good . . . Miss . . . ?"

"Tell him Venetia," said Miss Tay carefully.

"Yes, miss," said the man, turning coldly and taking yet another flight of stairs to his employer's chamber.

Venetia imagined Ferdy's face, for she could certainly hear his voice.

"What? Venetia? Here? Are you daft, man?" A moment later he was pulling on his dark-blue cutaway coat over his intricately embroidered blue silk waistcoat and charging down the stairs.

"Venetia!" he exclaimed when he had executed this feat and taken her by her shoulders. "You shouldn't be here! Good Lord, you must know that!"

"Ferdy . . . I have to talk to you, in private."

"Should have sent word. I would have come to you. Venetia, I've got to get you out of here. Did anyone see you come up?"

She shook her head dolefully. "Ferdy . . . this can't wait. As long as I am here . . ."

"No! Can't take that chance. The longer you are here the worse it would look." He took her arm and went to the door. His man was before him, opening it wide, and he was pulling her along with him down the stairs to the street below. When they reached the curbing she rounded on him in some exasperation.

"Oh, hang it all, Ferdy, listen to me!"

He turned then, his consternation written across his face. "So I will . . . but away from here."

"No, now! There is no one about, and I must tell you. Ferdy, an exciseman . . . *a dragoon came to Ingram Place today!*"

"You don't mean it! Blister it! He actually went to the squire?"

"Well, no, I intercepted him. Groomsby was clever enough to tell him the squire was unwell—which he is—and Ferdy, you know, don't you?"

"Confound Gilly! I've had a lively dread of this from the moment he started in on . . . well, never mind that. Damn, but I've had a feeling it would come to this!" Ferdy was moved to ejaculate.

"So then you do know. Ferdy, you must find him. Oh, Ferdy, he has been doing it for me, thinking to set us up in London. We can't let him get caught."

"I know, Van." He put a heartening arm around her. "Don't worry."

"Yes, but I just know they mean to set a trap for Gilly. I think tonight somewhere near the inlet that touches Ingram land."

"Do they? What makes you think so?"

"I don't know . . . just something in the dragoon's tone," she said, recalling the officer's expression. "Oh, Ferdy . . ."

"Hush now. It's probably all a hum. Why would they come to you and take a chance on your suspecting them of laying a trap?" He shook his head. "Odds are it's for another night."

"I don't know, Ferdy."

"Right, then, let's go over to the stable and fetch our horses."

"I have to get back to Ingram Place," she said doubtfully.

"So you shall. I think I know where I can find Gilly."

"Do you? Where?"

"Berwick. Undoubtedly he is with that grinning flasker crew of his." He saw the expression his unguarded words had evinced and immediately gave her shoulders a squeeze. "Heigh-ho, love, don't think I mean any scandal to touch my future brother-in-law?"

"Ferdy," she stopped him, "if you help us, you help as a friend . . . nothing more!"

He looked at her a long moment and suddenly released a short, boyish laugh. "Just testing."

"Right. That over with . . . we must hurry."

"Yes, and hope that no one has seen you coming out of my lodgings," he said, taking a quick glance around before leading her around the bend in the street to the stables.

However, someone had seen them, all too well. Lord Westbourne had stopped his horse abruptly when his gray eyes discovered Ferdy pulling Venetia down the steps of what was definitely a man's lodgings. What had Venetia been doing there with Ferdy? He watched. His mind was in a frenzy of thought with the information he had gained at the Preventive Station. Ferdy and Venetia conversed excitedly at the curbing, and

Taylor from an excellent vantage point observed as he dismounted and led his horse behind a vender's vegetable wagon.

He saw them head for the village stables and decided the situation called for additional surveillance on his part as he remounted his horse and went cautiously in pursuit.

"Uncle, may I speak with you?" It was Francine. She had received permission to enter her uncle's room, but she stood timidly at its door, for he looked as though more than that she wouldn't get from him.

He glanced at her and sighed. "I suppose you mean to . . . so don't stand there like a mouse! Good God, girl! Come in, come in."

She did and took up a chair near his bedside, where she looked doubtfully at him. "Uncle . . . I know it is your wish to have me married to one of your nephews . . ."

"You're wrong, child. That's not my wish at all." He was growing tired, so tired, these days, and all he could think about was Gussie, but there was more he had to say to Francine, so he took in a long draft of air. "Look . . . I still know what goes on in my own house. My people have always been a faithful crew, and I can still see . . . so don't think I didn't know at once that neither of my nevvies would do for you. Fact is, think you would drive them half-mad within the first year . . . they've needs you know nothing about." He saw her take affront and laughed caustically. "Never mind that. What matters is that Venetia has to take one of 'em."

She had risen for a moment, and her hands clasped one another at her waist. "Uncle ... I don't understand ... your will ..."

"Ha! Fooled all of you with that, didn't I?" He shook his head. "But it hasn't served. That gal of Gussie's has a mite too much blood in her! Can't be bought ... and I may have to call it off soon, but whatever I do, however I handle it, I want your word you'll not breathe a word of this. And don't think I'd take your word unless I knew you had cause to keep it!"

"Why, Uncle, I ..."

"Hush, girl! There isn't many a woman that can hold her tongue unless she has good enough reason, and if you want permission to marry that rascal of yours, you'll hold your tongue!"

She went toward her uncle and sat upon the bed, her face a mask of astonishment. "Uncle ... how did you know?"

"He was up here to see me this morning, right after he left you. Just waltzed in here and told me straight out that he meant to marry you with or without my consent. Like him. He is a bloody hothead and will no doubt end badly one of these days, but I like him all the same. Have a mind to give you two me blessing."

She moved to throw her arms around him but he waved her off desperately. "Don't do that, girl! Here ... stop it, I say!"

"Oh, but Uncle ... you have made me the happiest ... and he won't end badly. He'll change ... I know his spirits are such that they often lead him into ..."

"Hold there, child! Look, I've left you be all

these years and I'm too old and too tired to start meddling now, but don't you marry him if you mean to change him. You'll end with a stranger, and then neither of you will be happy."

She studied her uncle for a long moment. "You know, Uncle, Venetia has been saying to me that you have a heart under all your stiffness. I wasn't sure I believed her . . . but now I do."

"Go on. I don't have to listen to this fustian. Go on, get out of here!"

She dropped a kiss upon his forehead, laughed to see him wipe it away. "Till later then, my dearest Uncle."

"Good God! Don't be toad-eating at me, child, or I'll go off in an apoplexy!" He watched as she went to his door and called after her, "Mind now . . . not a word!"

"It is a promise," she said softly and left him to his thoughts.

Westbourne waited until Ferdy headed his horse down the Pike toward Berwick. Venetia turned back toward Ingram Place, and Westbourne made himself known. He entered the pike from a side avenue after quickly skirting around, as he did not wish Venetia to know he had seen her.

Venetia's green eyes went from the familiar horse to its rider, and she felt her heart take an extra beat. He was riding up to her, so she slowed her mare down to a rising trot and waited for him to bring his horse abreast.

"Hello," she said as best as she could muster.

"Good afternoon, Miss Tay. Are you riding back to the house?"

"Why, yes," she answered carefully.

"Good. We'll ride together." He waited for a moment and said in a bland voice, "Doing errands in the village?"

"Of a sort," she answered easily, and then cocking her head and glinting her green eyes at him, "And you?"

"Oh, visiting a friend of mine . . . new to your area . . . he is stationed at the Preventive Building. In charge of it, really."

Venetia nearly choked. She managed to maintain her outward composure and look away from him in time to avoid an overhanging branch from knocking her hat off.

"Careful," his lordship warned.

She looked at him. "Yes, I shall try to be."

Innuendoes. Well, if she meant to play with such things, he would too. But perhaps he could turn things around. It had been, after all, his initial behavior that had set the pattern for this day. "Had a notion," he said and glanced at her sideways, "of taking up Ferdy's invitation to drop by his lodgings. Thought he might wish to go into Berwick and find out about the pugilism match intended for tomorrow." He sighed audibly. "But I must have just missed him."

She sucked in air and avoided his eye. So he knew. Of course he knew. Sly thing. Why didn't he just come out and say what he thought of her? Well, she would teach him that she was no missish thing to be thrown into a swoon, "Oh, did you stop by there? So did I. Ferdy told me he plans to ride over to Berwick. Perhaps you can turn about and catch up to him?" She said it with wondrous sweetness.

He looked at her full, and she turned to find his eyes boring through her. "Brummell would have applauded you, my precious. I think that you are one of a kind, but then, perhaps country proprieties have relaxed since I was last here and admitting to an indiscretion is now the present mode?"

"Don't be absurd. I broke all the rules today," she said, "so think what you will."

"I think, my love, that you had reason." He was serious now; he wanted her to confide in him. "Perhaps I can help."

She wanted to tell him everything. She wanted to throw it on his very strong shoulders and allow him to handle it. Too much was happening, and she wasn't sure she could cope with it properly and save Gilly. She started, "I . . . you see . . ." and then she looked away.

"Venetia," he said softly. More than anything at that moment he wanted her to commit her trust to him. "If you should find that there is something beyond your ken to control, please believe me, I am here for you."

She looked at him sharply. What new thing was this? Oh, faith, she wanted to believe him. Every instinct told her that this was so. Logic told her it was not. They had been antagonists. They had sparred and countered. Why would he suddenly take it into his head to help her? "Thank you," she said, her pride forming her words. "If I need help . . . there is Ferdy."

"Yes, of course, I was forgetting Ferdy," said his lordship on a dry note. She alone had the ability to spark his ire. "A suitor worthy your trust . . . but Venetia . . . not your hand." He couldn't help adding that last.

"Stop it! One moment you think the vicar, Ferdy . . . probably even your cousin, all too good for my scheming clutches . . . and the next . . . oh . . . I don't know or care what you think!" With which she gave her horse leg and cantered off.

Westbourne could have caught up to her, but he didn't. Instead he watched her gallop off in some thoughtfulness. He had something to admit to himself as he watched her retreating form, for he had received his facer at last! He had hoped to bolster her spirits, but had failed, and why? Hadn't he behaved the cad to her these last few days? Why should she trust him? There was no reason on earth that she should, but damnation, before he was finished she would, she most definitely would.

Venetia was near to tears. Could Ferdy help? Would Gilly halt the pickup tonight? Were the excisemen setting a trap, and had she unwittingly taken a bait?

Westbourne? Lord, but he was confusing her, constantly throwing her into a frenzy of emotion, and deuce take him, why didn't he follow her if he cared? Because he didn't care! And more than anything else this made her want to cry!

Chapter Eighteen

Charles had spent a most frustrating morning. He had wanted to pursue his heady courtship of Venetia and go to his uncle with the results. Instead, he had discovered that she was nowhere to be found. An inquiry at the stables elicited the information that she had taken her mare out for a run to the village on an errand. Impatient to be with her, he saddled one of his uncle's horses and took to the road, hoping to intercept her on her way home. As he turned off the drive she nearly barreled into him.

Venetia saw something as she took the turn in the drive sharply and swerved her horse before pulling the mare up. Charles's horse spooked to the left, and she called out in some concern, "Are you all right?"

He laughed. "Yes, and thank you, that is the

most excitement I have had since you left here earlier. I was just coming to find you." He turned and trotted his horse up to her, thinking she looked devilishly handsome in her riding habit. She was flushed, and once again he thought it wouldn't be so very bad calling Venetia Lady Iverness. "Come on, then, I'll race you to the stables."

"Done!" She laughed and sent her horse off once again. They reached their destination very much out of breath and laughing before either one gave in, and it was with brighter spirits that Venetia said, "I think you have it by a nose, my lord."

"Yes, but then my horse was fresh, wasn't he?" His lordship took his win gallantly and hopped off the animal to come around and help Venetia dismount. She slid off the sidesaddle and landed very neatly in his arms, and he held her there.

"My lord," she said, gently rebuking him, "I am off, thank you, so you needn't worry that I might fall."

"Temptress!" he said on a soft laugh. Egad, but he was actually enjoying this courtship. He took her hand as the groom came hurrying out of the barn to take up the reins of their horses.

They walked a bit in silence, with Venetia wondering how she would extricate her hand from his, for she had tried to withdraw her gloved extremity without success. She stopped him, tugged out of his hold and said easily, "I fancy I need not be led to the house. I know the way."

He laughed and took her hand up and this time drew her arm through his. "Venetia . . . allow me, for I don't mean to give you up to the house, not yet."

"But Charles, I haven't been up to see the squire, and I do want to visit with him. He will be wondering where I am."

"And I am certain Groomsby will tell him you are with me, which should please him immensely. You do want to please him, don't you?"

"Oh, Charles ... you really are a charmer." She laughed.

"Charming enough to win you, Venetia?"

"Charming enough, I imagine, to win any maid," she said evasively.

"I don't want any maid. I want you."

"Me? No, you want your uncle's estates ... and there is nothing wrong with that. But Charles, I am afraid I can't fall in with you and my uncle," she said seriously.

Charles decided he was going to have to use his trump card. It hadn't taken much deducing to decide that young Tay was involved in a lark of sorts that had brought him under the excisemen's suspicions. The preventive officer today had put the idea into his head, and Gilly had fed the possibility only last night. He couldn't be certain, of course, but he could try a bluff and see what it would do.

"Venetia ... you might say I am a desperate man. There are things I would now consider doing that would never have crossed my mind before. Marriage is one of those things. Marriage to you makes the notion palatable. I shan't be such a very bad husband ... and my first duty to you would be to protect your brother." It was carefully said.

She stopped and looked at him full. "What do you mean?"

"I think you know what I mean. Of course, if Gilly weren't about to become my brother-in-law, I might consider it my duty to advise the preventive men about my observations *last night*." There, he had played his hand. He saw her eyes widen with fright. He heard her intake of air, and felt a moment's pulse of conscience. However, he quickly reminded himself that he had no choice. His life was at stake here.

"Charles, are you threatening me?" she said on a breathless note.

"No, my pretty . . . merely persuading you with every . . . er . . . weapon at my disposal!" He waited for a moment. "Shall I go and advise Uncle of our glad tidings?"

"Charles, I beg of you . . . don't do this thing to me. I . . . I don't love you."

He touched her cheek. "I know . . . but I shan't be so very hard to take, and in the end, my dear, we shall allow one another our amusements." His meaning was clear.

She wanted to run from him and did indeed back away. He held her fast. "Answer me, Venetia. Do I tell my uncle that we shall be wed?"

"No . . . oh no . . . Charles . . ."

"Then I am afraid I shall have to . . ."

"No . . . at least give me some time."

"What is this?" It was a strong, very magnetic voice, and both Venetia and Charles turned sharply around to discover Westbourne hovering, towering, frowning above them.

Venetia had no idea why she did it, but she took a stumbling step forward and landed neatly in Westbourne's arms. She wanted to tell him everything; instead, she said in a whisper, "Don't, Taylor . . ."

Charles frowned at his cousin darkly. "Do you know, cuz, that you are momentarily quite *de trop?* I am proposing to Venetia, and I find you very much in the way."

Westbourne looked down into Venetia's bright-green eyes and found there the checked tears. What was this? "Venetia . . ." He said her name tenderly. "Will you give him your answer, or shall I?"

"Stop . . . Taylor, you don't understand." She turned to Charles. "I will answer you in the morning, Charles. Don't ask for more than that."

"Very well, I will wait till the morning. But Venetia . . . I will have my answer then. You understand?"

She nodded, felt a sob choke her as she held it in her throat, and a moment later she was pulling out of Westbourne's arms and rushing toward the house. Incongruous that Charles should expect an answer while Westbourne held her? None of the players in the scene seemed to dwell on that overly much.

Taylor turned on his cousin, and his voice was a low and most ominous breath of air. "I don't know what you have said to her, I don't know why she is in such a state, but mark me well, Charles, Venetia Tay will never be Lady Iverness!"

"Don't you think so, dearest cuz?" returned Charles softly. "I know in your circle there are some who think you omniscient, but this time you may be wrong." He laughed shortly then. "Ah yes, you will find yourself very much out in this case." His chuckle was brought back to Westbourne on the trailing breeze, and Taylor watched his cousin leave in some tribulation.

It was definitely time he visited with his uncle. There was more here than met the eye, and one way or another he meant to handle it, but first, the squire was going to have to face certain facts!

In Berwick, there stood an old seaman's inn, whose weathered signboard depicted it as the Lost Ship's Inn. It had a look of a building that was seeing its last days. Within its warped and worm-eaten walls, fish nets were used to hide the peeling paint and rough-hewn rafters gave the appearance of maintaining the ceiling. On a windy night the entire building creaked, and often did a seaman take a bet as to the chances of the Ship's Inn's making it through the night.

In the darkest corner sat three fellows. One was garbed in the fashion of a young dandy, the second looked like a careless country blood and the third, a seedy bruiser whose occupation might have had something to do with the sea. The fashionable gentleman was in the process of gulping down a bumper of ale. This he did because of extreme agitation of nerves and not because the inn was famed for its brews. He put down the empty pewter with something of a bang and turned his bright-eyed gaze from the carelessly garbed young gentleman to the bruiser. "Tell him, won't you? Tell him you have got to call it off tonight!"

"Eh now, guv . . . Gilly 'ere . . . well, if ee says we go, we go."

"Ferdy! Calm down, will you? Granted, we shall have to lie low for a while. The dragoon's appearing now at Ingram Place means there is a leak in our group. But the goods that are on the squire's land . . . thunder and turf, man, should I just leave them there for the revenuers to pick up?"

"No, but . . ."

"Ferdy, we are going after the contraband tonight. But instead of taking it by sea, which is what the dragoons will think, we will take it off by land." He turned to the bruiser. "You had better go off and gather around the men. We'll need a wagon and we'll need a cover."

"Aye then, young'un. Yer've done right by us this far . . . guess we'll go the distance wit' ye."

Ferdy and Gilly watched the bruiser lift his large form out of the wooden chair and amble off before turning to one another. Ferdy attempted a new line of attack. "Gilly . . . what about Venetia? You can't put her through this."

Gilly frowned. "Well, maybe . . . just maybe we can make what I've saved carry us through a London Season."

"That is not what I mean!" snapped Ferdy. "I mean tonight. She will worry herself sick if you are a party to this thing. Damn, Gilly, you aren't in a cricket match!"

Gilly drew a long breath and studied his friend's harried expression. Things had, of course, gone too far. He had never meant to get as involved as he had done in the last few weeks, and he had never meant to worry Venetia. There was, however, nothing for it. "Ferdy, just how do I make you understand?" He touched his friend's shoulder. "Listen to me. The contraband ... we stored it last night on Ingram land."

"Dash it, Gilly ... you didn't!"

"What do you think I have been saying? A cutter was due, and we hadn't gotten close enough to the Berwick inlet. So we stopped at Ingram Place and unloaded lest she haul us about."

"Gilly!"

"Shut up, do. It wasn't the first time we have used that particular hole ... and I rather thought it could be the last. Damn, Ferdy, it will have to be the last."

"Gilly, what are we going to do?"

"We are going to have to get the goods off by land—haven't you been listening, you noddy? And we are going to have to do it tonight, before the contraband is discovered."

"Gilly, how did they ... what I mean is, why do they suspect you?"

Gilly eyed him. "I have been using a very pretty little bit of muslin as go-between for our crew and the Dutchman. I just wonder if she is tipping us false ... playing both sides."

"I wonder how much she has told the dragoons, then ... and whether or not she has pointed a finger at you, Gilly."

"I tell you what, Ferdy ... let us go pay her a visit and find out."

"Right, then, and what's more, Gilly, I don't mean to let you flounder tonight! Shabby thing to do to a friend. A daft fellow you are, but a friend all the same. Mean to help."

Gilly got to his feet with a laugh. "And pray, old boy, how do you mean to do that?"

"Have a plan."

"Do you? Upon my soul, Ferdy, getting into the spirit of the lark?"

" 'Tis no lark, my friend. This is a smoky business, but I mean to do what I can to save your neck."

Gilly put an arm about him as they walked out of their notorious surroundings into the afternoon sun. "Do you, Ferdy? That's a buck, but tell me, what do you have in mind?"

Groomsby attempted to deter Westbourne with an apologetic inclination of his head and a gentle reminder that the squire was still not quite up to receiving visitors unannounced.

"Don't worry, Groomsby, I will announce myself," said Westbourne grimly as he swept past the retainer and took the hall down to the squire's room.

A knock at the squire's door elicited a hollow silence, and his lordship repeated it. Nothing. He wasn't ever one to give up easily, and he did not do so now. He set up a pounding that shook the door.

The squire sat up and shouted in a raspy voice, "Sneck up there! Damn . . . do you mean to break it in? Who is it?"

Westbourne opened the door and said lightly, "See for yourself, Uncle. I mean to have a word with you."

"Do you, by God! Whether I wish it or no?"

"That's right," said Westbourne, moving into

the room, taking up a chair, reversing it and straddling it with purpose.

"Capital!" the squire returned sardonically. "A fine thing it is when a man is so used on his deathbed!"

"And I have had quite enough of that too, you old faker! Deathbed indeed. You have used a ruse to get us up here and under your thumb, but I am afraid that I am calling an end to the game ... here and now!"

"Are you, Westbourne? Are you indeed? And what game is that?" snapped the squire with a sharp movement of his head. His nightcap fell forward over his eyes, and he pushed it backward with a gruff complaint as he stared appreciatively at his nephew.

"Let's not bandy words, Uncle. At first ... when you first announced your demands, I thought I would sit back and amuse myself by watching, but I am afraid this sport has turned ugly."

"Eh, what's that? Ugly? What do you mean?"

"To start with, I am not interested in your inheritance. I inherited quite a fortune some time ago ... which I haven't yet had the need to own publicly. It's been a well-guarded secret of mine, a whim of sorts to keep quite silent about it and avoid using it until such time as I had set my father's estates back in order."

"I know all about that! Young fool ... I have my ways of finding out what you young 'uns are at! I'm old and I'm tired, but I'm not stupid!"

"Then why did you ... ? I don't understand."

"Don't you? Knew you would play along for the sport ... and I wanted you to take a good look at

Venetia. When you were here three years ago you were too much caught up in your grief to notice her." He sighed. "Thought my plan might serve to make you see her . . . really see her."

Westbourne smiled enigmatically, and there was a strange light in his gray eyes. "See her? Yes, it served to that end. I have seen her well enough, but then so has Charles . . . to a point."

"Ah, bah! You don't know Gussie's Venetia if you think she'll have Charles!"

"Ah, but Charles is a determined man . . . and would make use of any means at hand to get what he wants."

The squire frowned. "Now, Taylor . . . I know you and your cousin don't get on. Charles may be many things . . . but he isn't really bad at bottom."

"Then don't force him to do what would go against his nature. Charles is desperate. He needs to inherit."

The squire cut him off. "What the deuce do you think I've done anyway? I thought you saw through my game. Don't you know, the only heir I've put down in my will is Charles! You don't need it. Francine will do well enough with Whitney. And that leaves only Charles. Damnation, did you think I would let m'sister's son go to debtors' prison?"

"Then tell him. Tell him now."

"No . . . I can't do that yet. I've got my whims just as you have yours, and it suits me to keep Charles in the dark just a mite longer." He eyed Westbourne. "Well, Taylor . . . do you mean to have my Gussie's Venetia?"

"I do," said Westbourne quietly but with resolute determination. "I would move heaven and join it to hell to have Venetia Tay."

The squire smiled. "Ha! And will she have you." Because Westbourne did not answer, he frowned. "Well . . . will she?"

"I can't answer you, Uncle, but I have a feeling you will have your answer from Venetia . . . in the morning!"

Chapter Nineteen

The evening was proving to be for Venetia a te-
diously long one. She had not gone down to dinner,
feigning illness. Therefore the dinner party had
consisted of the squire's nephews, Francine and
George Whitney. Gilly had not yet returned, and
a message from Ferdy had not stilled her fears. In
that missive he had said only that he had located
Gilly, nothing more. She wanted to scream. Instead
she had paid a short visit to her uncle. He had behaved oddly, and she was surprised to find him
almost affectionate. That was certainly not part of
his outward exterior, and she had not expected it.
He had not mentioned either Charles or Westbourne, and he had not pressed her about the
question of her marriage. Odd.

What to do? What would Gilly be doing? What
was Charles going to do? And Taylor ... how

could she have allowed herself to begin to think of Taylor . . . the way she thought of him now? Drat it all, everything was falling apart around her, and she wasn't sure how she would put things together.

A knock sounded at her door, and she looked up from the low-burning coals in her hearth. She had bathed earlier and had sat in her silk wrapper by the fire to dry her hair. It glittered in white-gold profusion around her head. She got to her feet with a long sigh and padded gently to the door, which she opened only a crack.

Westbourne pushed it open wider and entered the room. "May I come in for a moment?"

She grimaced, but her heart beat rapidly. "I see that I really have no choice."

He took stock of her and nearly lost his breath. It took a moment of silence in which he composed himself and kept his hands at his sides. She noted that he was the best-looking man alive as she stared into his gray, very bright eyes.

"You do," he said softly. "If you want me to go, I will. See, I have left the door open."

She saw; indeed, she still stood beside it and watched him move to the fire. She was still chilled and followed him there.

"You are the most arrogant . . . the coolest . . ." she started, and then looked away.

He had already dropped down to the hearth rug. His hand took hers and urged her down beside him. "Come, Venetia. We need to talk, you and I."

She looked at him a long moment. "You are being outrageous."

"Am I? We are well suited, then. Come, Venetia."

She wanted to. More than anything she wanted to drop down into his arms and let him command. She took a timid position opposite him and stared at the flames, avoiding his gaze. "What then did you wish to talk about?"

"About us, Venetia."

"Oh ho, so you have decided you need your uncle's inheritance after all?" She felt a sting of hurt. Here he was selling out . . . he wanted her, but for the wrong reason.

He laughed and took her shoulders, "I don't give a fig for the squire's estates, Venetia."

"Damnation!" snapped Charles from the doorway. "I thought perhaps this was your destination!"

"Go away, Charles," said Westbourne grimly without turning around.

"I will not." Charles took a step into the room. "I will have you know that you are toying with my future bride."

Westbourne straightened. "What the devil are you talking about?"

"Tell him, Venetia!" demanded Charles.

Venetia blushed. "It isn't decided yet, Charles."

"No, but it will be in the morning, and you gave me reason to believe your answer would be in the affirmative!" retorted Charles. His words were chosen particularly to spark Westbourne's jealousy and send him off. He chose them well.

Westbourne jumped to his feet. His gray eyes hardened. "I see," he said on a low note.

Venetia was close to tears. "Taylor . . ." She couldn't say anything; indeed, how could she? What should she say? Charles is blackmailing me—he knows my brother has been playing at smuggler and means to inform against him unless I marry him? How could she?

Westbourne heard the plea in her voice and was not immune. He looked from her to his cousin doubtfully. There was something here he was missing. What did Charles have over her? Damn! Did Charles somehow suspect Gilly? How could he? Well, well. Was he teasing Venetia with that? He smiled suddenly and bent to take Venetia's chin in his fingers. "Don't worry, my love. In the morning you will be announcing your engagement, but it won't be to Charles." He put a finger over her lips to silence her.

"Trust me." With this he left the room, ignoring Charles's remarks at his back. There was still a great deal to be handled this evening.

"Get out of my room, Charles," said Venetia, her brow up.

He started to object, thought better of it and backed off to the door. "Goodnight then, my dearest."

"Charles . . ." Venetia could not help saying.

"Yes, my bride?"

"Go to the blackest part of Hades," she said, smiling.

"I probably shall, you know," he answered, grinning, and was gone.

Venetia could not help thinking even at that her most dismal hour that he was certainly a charmer. Had circumstances been different, he would have been an amusing friend.

"Gawd! Get off me foot, ye snirp!" hissed one seaman as he heaved a keg onto the wagon.

Gilly chided them in a whisper, "Keep your mummers clapped, or do you mean for the dragoons to find us after all?" He hoisted a flask onto his back and moved toward the wagon with it. The work was taking longer than he had anticipated.

" 'Tis a prime twig it is when a sea worthy has to do landlubbers' work!" complained another.

"Aye," agreed Gilly with a grin, "and a prime thing indeed when a gentleman has to hoist a load with such as you!"

This set some of the men to laughing, and once again Gilly had to tell them to hush, then to another who was standing about looking at nothing in particular, "Noddy! Quit your goggling and get to work, unless you have a fancy to have your neck stretched in the morning!"

Ferdy gave an excellent impression of a young man foxed out of his mind as he raised his pewter of ale and bumped it with the dragoon across from him. "Good stuff, this," he said as he swayed.

"Aye . . ." But the dragoon shook his head. "Has to be me last, though. Meeting with Crail . . . coming by for me . . . and off we go."

"Off you go? Where would you be wanting to go?" slurred Ferdy beautifully.

"Nowhere . . . but has to, you know. Duty."

"Duty. No, no, duty to finish this good ale. Can't waste it on fools."

"Aye, that's a fact," agreed the dragoon in red uniform, "but Crail now . . . he thinks we best be meeting with our men. Went to fetch a regular squadron, he did . . . and off we gooo."

"Off you gooo . . ." repeated Ferdy stupidly.

Privately, he patted himself on his back for his performance. "Where?"

The dragoon leaned forward and held Ferdy's neck. "Secret," said the dragoon.

Ferdy cleaned his eye from the officer's spray. "Secret. Mustn't tell me, then."

"No . . . but you're a friend. Can't keep a secret from a friend."

"No, can't do that."

"That's right. So . . . there you are."

"There I am. Where?" pursued Ferdy.

"Shhh. Ingram Place."

"Ingram Place? Why?"

"Catch him."

"Catch him?" repeated Ferdy.

"Aye . . . that young Tay."

"Know what?" said Ferdy suddenly.

"What?"

"Think I've had a bit too much ale . . . think I'll go out back and . . . and . . ." He gave every indication that he was in a hurry to find the outdoors.

The dragoon blinked as Ferdy vanished. Now, what sort of a drinking partner was that? He shook his head and awaited the arrival of his superior officer.

Ferdy took to horse. Gilly would have to be warned. Fervently he hoped that the wagon was on its way south by now. Damn, but what if Crail took it into his head to search the wagon? Well, perhaps the false bottom would serve to hide the contraband in the dark. Perhaps.

* * *

Venetia couldn't stand it any longer. She slipped into her breeches, pulled on her linen shirt and her dark hooded cloak. She was still pulling on her boots as she opened her door and peeped into the hallway. No one about. Good. Hurriedly she sped out the back way. She had to go down to the river and see if Gilly was there and if everything was in order.

Her heart pounded as she raced down the lawn. The sound of a horse brought her to a dead stop. Who was it? Oh God . . . a dragoon? The rider drew up short in front of her and said her name on a low, breathless note. "Van . . . that you?"

"Ferdy. Thank goodness," she managed.

"Here . . . take my hand," he said, reaching for her.

She put her foot in the stirrup and allowed him to hoist her up behind him, "What is it, Ferdy? What is happening? Where is Gilly?"

"No time," he said and spurred his horse forward. They cut down the neat stretch of lawn to the river below and stopped. There was total silence, and Ferdy called out, "Gilly . . . 'tis me."

A hushed group of oaths emitted as Gilly stepped out of the forest into the moonlight. "Damn, Ferdy . . . gave you the password." He then saw his sister. "Thunder and turf! Van . . . what the . . .?"

"No time," repeated Ferdy, this fact erasing nearly all others. "Gilly . . . no time . . . they are coming with an entire squadron. Crail went to fetch more men, and they are coming here. Gilly, they will cut off the pike."

Gilly swore beneath his breath. "Well, we'll just

have to get moving. We are all loaded. So if we can just get on the road . . ."

"Gilly . . . where is the wagon?" said Van.

"Not far from here, near the drive, ready to move out."

"Well then, move it out!" snapped Ferdy. "Ain't you been listening?"

"Right, then . . . and maybe we'll get on the south road before they get to the pike. They will think we mean to take the road to Berwick. So perhaps . . ."

"Hurry, Gilly . . ." This from Venetia.

A few moments later, three seamen sat atop a wagon whose first level carried a small quantity of sheered lamb's wool. Gilly rode at its fore, playing at scout; Ferdy and Van, riding double, were at its back.

"Get her home," shouted Gilly to his friend.

"No, I won't go," returned Venetia.

"You don't have any choice," snapped Gilly.

She slapped Ferdy's head. "Owww," he reacted.

"Don't you dare turn this horse about, Ferdy. I won't have it," said the lady.

At the intersection of the road and Ingram Drive, they were stopped by a tall and imposing figure. It was Westbourne.

"Hurry, Gilly . . . get this wagon out of sight!"

"Westbourne . . . what are you doing?" returned Gilly in some amazement.

"The dragoons are but five minutes away, and when they intercept a wagon coming off Ingram land, it will be *my* wagon, not yours, and when, suspicious, they decide to follow that wagon, it will be my wagon not yours, which will leave yours free to take the south road."

"How . . . where . . ." started Gilly.

Westbourne indicated, with a movement of his head, a wagon presided over by two men waiting in the road. "I will explain everything to you later, Gilly . . . now, may I suggest you hurry?"

Gilly went into action, and some moments later, his wagon, his smugglers and its load were secreted in Ingram woods. While this was being accomplished, Westbourne moved to Ferdy and said quietly, "May I relieve you of your charge and take her back to the house?"

"Good notion, that! Been trying to tell her, but I daren't open my mouth for fear of my life," Ferdy grinned.

"I don't want to leave Gilly," whispered Venetia.

"It would be better, safer for him, if we were out of sight," Westbourne answered gently.

She slid off the back of Ferdy's horse and came over to Westbourne, who hoisted her up not at his back, but in his arms. "How is that?" he asked, smiling.

"Dashed uncomfortable," she answered. "Now, rogue . . . explain yourself!"

"Ho! Listen to the vixen. Here she is playing at smuggling with a scamp of a brother and as wicked a crew as ever I clapped eyes on, and she wants an explanation from me!"

She laughed. "You know what I mean. How did you know . . . how did you arrange . . . oh, Westbourne . . ." She sank against his chest and thought she never wanted to be anywhere else but in his arms.

He stroked her head. "I knew that something was amiss this morning, when Crail was at the house. Decided to visit the station and see his superior officer, who turned out to be a good friend of mine. He confided in me, and I am ashamed to say that I used what he told me to devise a plan. I rather suspected Gilly would move his shipment out by land. It was what they hoped he would do, and my friend knows all about false bottoms in wagons. So there was only one thing to do. Give them a wagon they couldn't find anything but silks, teas and spices on . . . tease them with a documented flask or two so that they would follow the wagon to its destination."

"Taylor, you are brilliant," she said, delighted with him. He stopped his horse at the stable, dismounted and took her into his arms and off his horse. He gave his animal a sharp tap on the rump and the horse went trotting into the stable, where the groom came quickly to fetch him.

He stopped Venetia as they approached the house and said gravely, "We will, of course, have to find some useful employment for that brother of yours in London, you know."

"We?" she said, feeling her knees go weak.

"Yes. I rather think the Home Office would be a good place for him to start."

"The Home Office?" she repeated dumbly.

"Hmmm . . . yes, I think that should do nicely. And by the by, I think it must be Venice, you know."

"Venice?"

"Venice," he repeated. "We can pay a visit on Byron and see what he is up to these days."

"We ... Venice? Oh no ... no ... Taylor ... you aren't asking me to marry you?" she cried in some distress.

"Well, of course I am, you little fool."

She started to run from him. How could he? This was terrible. She thought he was the one man who would hold out against her uncle, and here he was succumbing like any other. She wanted to cry.

He held her fast. "Venetia ... my own precious ... what the devil is wrong?"

"How can you ask? You are proposing to me to get your hands on the squire's money ... to outdo Charles, no doubt."

He cut her off by taking her into his arms and kissing her long, hard and sweetly. When he let her up for air, it was to whisper in her ear, "Do you believe that, Venetia? Do you really believe that?"

"I don't want to. I want to stay here in your arms and think, believe, that you want me ..."

"Confound it, woman! Can't you see that I want you? Fire and brimstone, Venetia ... I have been wanting you since the first moment I saw you."

"No, the first moment you saw me was three years ago, and you didn't want me three years ago," she pointed out.

"I didn't see you then," he said softly. "That was the year of Waterloo."

"Oh." She bit her lip and then shook her head. "Oh, Taylor ... if only the squire hadn't done this to us with his will. It taints everything."

He laughed and held her fast. "The squire isn't leaving me a groat. It all goes to Charles, regardless of whom Charles means to marry. You see, a relative left me a tidy sum a while back, and I am . . . er . . . quite a wealthy man, you know."

"What?" shrieked Venetia. "All this time . . . you and the squire knew this . . ." She started to struggle in some earnest, for she had a notion of landing her sweet love a feisty kick to his shin. However, his kiss sent this notion to perdition, and as she came up for air a second time, she said in some confusion, "Taylor . . . Taylor . . . I don't understand. Everything is in such disorder . . ."

He kissed her eyes, her nose, her lips. "Ah, but such sweet disorder, my dearest, my only love!"